Annie's Quilted Mysteries™

A DEADLY PATTERN

ELIZABETH PENNEY

Annie's®
AnniesFiction.com

A Deadly Pattern
Copyright © 2014 Annie's.

The characters and events in this book are fictional, and any resemblance to
actual persons or events is coincidental.

Library of Congress-in-Publication Data
A Deadly Pattern / by Elizabeth Penney
p. cm.
I. Title
                    2014940305

AnniesFiction.com
800-282-6643
Annie's Quilted Mysteries
Series Creator: Shari Lohner
Series Editors: Shari Lohner, Janice Tate, and Ken Tate

10 11 12 13 14 | Printed in China | 9 8 7 6 5 4 3 2 1

There is nothing as eloquent as a rattlesnake's tail.
—Navajo Proverb

one

As the plane circled the Flagstaff airport in preparation for landing, Emma Cotton gazed at the dry, mountainous landscape with interest. She'd never been in the American Southwest, but thanks to another lead in the mystery of her friend Rose Peterson's death, she was headed for Sedona, Arizona, along with her best friend, Kelly Grace, and her aunt, Dottie Faye Sinclair.

The plane dipped and her stomach tightened. The thrill wasn't entirely caused by the thought of finding the killer once and for all. Flying was barely tolerable for Emma in large jetliners, and this one was tiny. Dottie Faye's motion sickness medicine had helped—somewhat.

"How you doing?" Kelly asked from the seat beside her, giving Emma's hand an encouraging squeeze. Emma attempted to smile; Kelly was not only her best friend, but also her partner at Cotton & Grace, a quilt design shop back in Mystic Harbor, Massachusetts. But Kelly wasn't fooled. "Hang in there. We're almost on the ground."

"I'm OK," Emma said through tight lips as the plane made its final descent. In the row ahead of them, Dottie Faye gave a pealing laugh. She'd spent the whole flight flirting with the tall man in a cowboy hat sitting across the aisle. Or rather, attempting to flirt. The man responded only in grunts or monosyllabic answers, Emma noticed. He must be one of the few men on the planet resistant to Dottie Faye's considerable charms.

"Do you want these?" Kelly asked, waving Emma's bag of airline peanuts. "I'm starved." At Emma's headshake, she ripped open the bag. "Don't forget that it's actually 2:30 in Boston. Lunch was hours ago."

"You're right," Emma agreed. She thought of their shop back in Mystic Harbor. Once again, they had left it in the capable hands of Kelly's mother, Maeve Quigley. "I hope things are going well at the store."

"After I call home to check in, I'll call Mom too." Unlike Emma and Dottie Faye, who were single, Kelly had a husband and two children, and she hated taking trips without them. "I really hope we can wrap this up quickly and get back before Easter weekend," she said. "I still have a lot to do with the whole family coming to our house this year." Her expression was fretful.

Emma hastened to reassure her. "We have more than a week to find Dakota and get her DNA," she said. "And your dinner's going to be wonderful. I'm looking forward to it." Since they had no other relatives nearby, Emma and Dottie Faye were included on the guest list for many of Kelly's family functions. Easter was no exception.

"I hope you're right," Kelly said, crumpling up the peanut bag. "So far none of our investigations have been simple or easy."

"No, but they've been interesting," Emma said wryly. She gave a sigh of relief and a whispered prayer of thanksgiving as the plane finally landed and taxied down the runway toward the gate. Crossing her fingers, she hoped she was right about the trip being a short one. They had very little to go on this time beyond the location of their suspect in Sedona, where she lived and worked. Dakota Longbone hadn't argued with Rose, like Kevin, or wanted to date her, like Colin. She had merely appliquéd an owl, the symbol of death in some Native American tribes, on her block for the class quilt. Until she learned its sinister meaning, Emma had thought the owl cute and harmless.

The DNA under Rose's fingernails came from a female. Maybe Dakota's owl was a warning or a threat after all.

"Bye, Buck," Dottie Faye caroled, waving at the man who sat near her in the plane. He tipped his hat at the trio and strode away from the gate. "He was so nice," Dottie Faye gushed. "And guess what? He's going to Sedona too." She gave Emma a meaningful look. "He's just a little older than you, Emma Jane. Good-looking too." In honor of their trip, Dottie wore a pink Western-style outfit that included a yoked shirt with mother-of-pearl snaps, jeans, and boots. Her belt featured a big oval silver buckle with a floral design. In contrast, Emma and Kelly were dressed for comfort, not style, in jeans, long-sleeved T-shirts, and sneakers.

"That's nice, Dottie Faye," Emma said, hoping they had seen the last of Buck. All she needed right now were more matchmaking attempts from Dottie Faye. "First we need to get our luggage and the rental car, and then we can get on the road to Sedona." Emma walked down the tiled hallway toward baggage claim. The other two fell into step.

"How far is it to Sedona?" Kelly asked, rubbing her midriff. "I don't think those peanuts are going to hold me until we get to the resort."

Emma was also feeling hunger pangs now that she was safely on the ground. "About thirty miles. Why don't you pick up sandwiches to go for all of us at that café over there? I'll wait for the luggage, and Dottie Faye can go ahead and get the rental car since it's in her name."

"Just let me freshen up first," Dottie Faye said, halting next to the women's room. She fluffed her towering blond locks, eyeing a pair of men in 10-gallon hats walking past. "I want to look my best, considering all the handsome gentlemen around here." Her Southern accent was getting thicker. "I just adore cowboys."

Kelly rolled her eyes at Emma as they followed Dottie Faye into the restroom. "Do you think Arizona is ready for Dottie Faye?" she whispered.

Emma snorted. "I think any cowboys in the vicinity better buckle up and hang onto their hats."

"And their guns," Kelly added. Dottie Faye had a rather alarming fondness for firearms of all sizes and types.

A short while later, Emma and Kelly stood on the sidewalk in front of the terminal waiting for Dottie Faye to arrive in the rental car. Beside them stood their modest suitcases, one each, and the pile of embossed pink leather luggage Dottie Faye had brought, including a makeup case and hatbox.

Kelly perched on the edge of a flower-filled planter and looked inside the bag of sandwiches. "If you don't mind, I'm going to start eating." She pulled out a paper-wrapped turkey sandwich loaded with vegetables and took an enormous bite. Emma was always amazed that Kelly could keep slim with her considerable appetite. Three inches shorter than Emma, Kelly didn't run or have daily yoga sessions the way Emma did to maintain her weight.

Emma remained standing, looking for Dottie Faye among the fleet of cars and taxis and shuttles rolling past the terminal.

The sun was brilliant in a deep blue sky, the light so bright that she had to put on her sunglasses. "I wish I had changed," she said, flapping the neck of her T-shirt. "It's getting hot."

"But it's a dry heat," Kelly quipped around a mouthful of sandwich. "Don't worry. The car will have AC." She opened a bottle of water and took a long swallow.

"I don't think we'll need it," Emma said. Even from a distance she spotted Dottie Faye's trademark hair behind the wheel of a red convertible Mustang with the roof down.

"Wow. Nice car," Kelly said as Dottie Faye pulled up in front of them. "I call shotgun."

"Isn't she pretty?" Dottie Faye said with a smug smile. "I got a free upgrade. We're gonna be riding in style."

Emma eyed the small back seat, thinking of her long legs. "Some of us are, anyway." She carted the luggage to the rear of the car and, with Kelly's help, managed to stuff most of it in. The hatbox and makeup case had to ride beside her in the back.

"Don't worry, Emma," Kelly said as Dottie Faye accelerated away from the curb. "I'll let you sit up here next trip." She handed Emma a sandwich and a bottle of water.

Emma smiled in amusement at the promise, turned her legs sideways for comfort, and after unwrapping her lunch, sat back to enjoy the ride and her first experience of Arizona.

The airport was on the outskirts of Flagstaff, so they quickly reached the city limits and headed south to Sedona. Dottie Faye turned onto scenic route 89A, which wound between partially wooded peaks and past striated cliffs bordering the road on both sides. The deeper into the mountains they drove, the more spectacular the views became, providing glimpses of the dramatic canyon lands surrounding Sedona.

When the grades grew steeper and sharp curves

appeared, Dottie Faye didn't slow down like the cautious drivers heading toward them. She sped up, taking corners like a racing champion. "Did I tell you about the time I had a job testing stock cars in North Carolina?" she yelled over the wind whipping past. "We drove those beauties over 100 miles per hour."

"You don't need to do that now," Kelly shouted, glancing nervously at the speedometer. "We're not in any hurry."

Thankfully for Emma and Kelly's nerves, they entered a particularly treacherous stretch of hairpin turns that forced even Dottie Faye to slow down. As the car's speed decreased, Emma heard the rumble of a loud, throaty engine behind them. She glanced over her shoulder to see a large, battered red pickup barreling their way. Shifting in her seat, she turned for a better look. The windshield was so dirty she could discern nothing of the driver's appearance except the distinctive outline of a cowboy hat—something just about everyone, male and female, seemed to wear in Arizona.

"What's that fellow doing?" Dottie Faye asked, her eyes on the rearview mirror as the truck continued to approach.

Kelly turned to look and her eyes widened in alarm. "I hope he hasn't lost his brakes or something."

The truck didn't hit them. Instead, it slowed as it moved closer, settling into a pattern of riding their bumper by matching their speed. When Dottie Faye sped up, he sped up. And the same when she braked.

"Can you see his license plate?" Dottie Faye asked Emma. "Something's not right."

Twisting around even further, Emma peered over the rear of the car at the truck's bumper, but it was so close she couldn't see the plate. When the driver backed off a trifle, she saw there wasn't one. Some states didn't require front plates, she knew, and right now that seemed like a really stupid law.

"He doesn't have a plate," Emma yelled. "Can you pull over and let him by?"

There wasn't an adequate shoulder to fully stop, so Dottie Faye eased up even more and edged over as far as she could.

The truck continued to shadow them despite the opportunity to pass.

Emma felt the cold trickle of sweat between her shoulder blades. The invisible driver in the menacing truck was targeting them. She sensed it.

Rounding a tight corner, with only a single metal railing protecting them from plunging down a deep ravine and into the canyon, the driver accelerated, smashing his truck into their bumper. *Bam!*

Kelly screamed. "Hang on, girls!" Dottie Faye yelled.

Emma closed her eyes and prayed as they went sailing toward the guardrail and oblivion.

two

Dottie Faye successfully avoided the guardrail and the plunge to certain death. But her correction sent them careening across the other lane, narrowly missing a propane truck and sending them shooting toward a rock wall. With another quick twist of the wheel, Dottie Faye had the Mustang on the proper side, tires screeching as the rear of the convertible fishtailed.

Emma squeezed her eyes closed and gripped the seat with both hands, bracing for another collision from behind. Daring to peek with one eye, she saw the red pickup roar pass them, endangering a line of oncoming traffic, and zoom away. The license plate was covered with mud, she noticed, making it impossible to read.

Was that deliberate, or is he just a drunk driver?

"You no-account Yankee fool!" Dottie Faye yelled, shaking her fist, as she rolled into a roadside overlook and braked sharply. To Dottie Faye, calling someone a Yankee was a severe insult.

A minivan holding a couple and several children pulled into the adjacent parking spot. They had been in the oncoming lane, and the truck had narrowly missed them. The man rolled down the driver's side window. "Are you ladies all right?" He pulled out a handkerchief and mopped his broad, balding head.

His wife put one hand to her chest. "My heart is still racing. That pickup almost hit us."

"He *did* hit us," Dottie Faye said grimly. She opened the car door and got out, followed by Kelly and Emma.

Emma's legs wobbled as her feet hit the ground, and she grabbed onto Kelly's arm for support. "My life flashed before my eyes," she said with a shudder.

Kelly's face was somber. "Dottie Faye, you saved us. That was some amazing driving. Just our luck to run into a drunk driver. "

Emma opened her mouth to share her theory that it might be the mysterious person who had been harassing them ever since they started investigating Rose's death. *But that's too far-fetched,* she thought. *How could our stalker know we're in Arizona?*

"I can't believe it," Dottie Faye cried. Emma and Kelly hurried to join her at the rear of the car. A tiny dent was all there was to show that the truck had hit them.

"It's a miracle," Kelly said.

The man shook his head. "Sure is. Someone up there must like you." He jabbed a thumb toward the cerulean sky.

Emma breathed a prayer of thanksgiving.

The brief chirp of a siren sounded, and they all looked up to see a blue-and-white Arizona highway patrol car pulling in, lights flashing.

"I called 911," the woman said. "I thought we should report that driver before he hurts someone." She scrambled out of the van and opened the side door to give the children some air.

"I hope he's at the bottom of a cliff!" Dottie Faye fumed. "Is that wrong?"

A burly young officer climbed out of the cruiser and walked over to the group. Dottie Faye gave him the story, embellished with arm gestures and exclamations about dangerous drivers who should be locked away for life. While they waited, Emma and Kelly perched on big boulders and looked out at the vista of multicolored rock formations and canyons stretching into the distance. The whistle of wind was the only sound—besides Dottie Faye's voice and the occasional car driving by. Far above, a turkey vulture soared gracefully on the wind currents.

"This is gorgeous," Kelly said, "now that I've calmed down enough to enjoy it."

Emma squinted at the striped rocks. "I'd love to make a quilt with those colors. Buff and ochre and sienna and vermillion."

Kelly snapped her fingers. "Back at the shop, I have a pattern that would be perfect. It's geometric, with a Native American feel. Nine diamonds on diamonds, three in each row, with contrasting triangle insets. They used those colors."

"That sounds fantastic." Emma pulled her phone out of her jeans pocket and took a few photos for a reminder of the idea.

After the policeman finished his report and left with a promise to look for the pickup driver, Dottie Faye said goodbye to the family and joined Emma and Kelly, her good spirits restored. Gazing at the view, she took a huge breath and flung her arms wide. "I can feel the positive energy already," she enthused.

"What are you talking about, Dottie Faye?" Emma asked.

"Don't you know that Sedona has four of those vortex things?" She made a swirling motion with one manicured hand. "The energy of the earth gathers there. You have to be a sensitive person to tap into it." She took another deep breath.

Emma and Kelly exchanged amused looks. "If you say so, Dottie Faye," Emma said. "You feel OK to drive or do you want one of us to take over? I mean, especially with all of those vortex things around."

Dottie Faye flapped her hand. "Shoot, I'm fine. It takes more than a li'l old crazy driver to scare a Southern gal. That was nothing. You should've seen those mountain passes in North Carolina we used to drag race on every Saturday afternoon." She laughed. "And of course there was moonshine involved. Not that I ever imbibed ...."

"Dottie Faye, you are something," Kelly said. Emma had to agree.

The rest of the journey passed without incident or another sighting of the pickup. On the way to the Radiance Resort, they drove along Sedona's main street, where the famous red rock cliffs loomed behind rows of low storefronts, gas stations, and restaurants. Emma spotted numerous art galleries and boutiques, many featuring Native American crafts. Dining ranged from casual to upscale, including everything from pizza to sushi.

While stopped at a light in front of a designer clothing shop, Dottie sighed. "I'm gonna love shopping in this town."

"I can see why they get so many visitors," Kelly said.

"It is gorgeous," Emma said.

"And looks like it's a lot of fun," Kelly added.

A short distance from the edge of downtown, Dottie Faye turned onto a side road that would take them to the resort nestled in the heart of a canyon. From what Emma had read online, Radiance was one of the most luxurious properties in Sedona. The amenities had sold Dottie Faye, who was footing the bill, and she justified the expense because Dakota Longbone often worked there as a speaker and guide.

A simple sign that read Radiance announced the entrance. After stopping at the gatehouse, they entered the canyon, a multi-acre spread surrounded by towering rock formations. Tan stucco buildings with rounded walls were set across the hillsides, tucked unobtrusively among cedars and pines and junipers. They reminded Emma of Native American cliff dwellings she'd seen in pictures, which she supposed was the idea—to help the resort blend into the landscape, instead of a jarring man-made intrusion. At the main building, Dottie Faye parked under the wide portico at the entrance. After two bellmen unloaded Dottie's luggage, they entered the hotel.

The spacious lobby's Southwestern decor was infused with elegant and modern touches. A number of guests waited to check in at the front desk, a polished mahogany expanse attended by two women and a man. Still others sat and chatted or read newspapers in the sleek black leather sofas and chairs set in groups here and there on the pale tan tiled floor. Flute music over the sound system set a pleasant mood, and the square chandelier lights hanging from the beamed ceiling cast a warm, flattering glow. But what caught the trio's interest was the display case along one wall. Each niche held a piece of Native American pottery.

Kelly sucked in a breath. "These are all antiques," she said, pointing to a card under one piece that read, *Hopi Canteen With Kachina, 1910*. The round, tan piece of pottery had a figure etched on the side in faded red and black. "What's a *kachina*, I wonder?"

"My dear lady, a *kachina* is a spirit being," a deep voice with a delightful English accent said. They turned to see a slender, short man with a pencil-thin mustache and slicked-back hair standing behind them. He wore the resort uniform of black pants, white dress shirt, and bolo tie consisting of a strand of black leather fastened with a silver slide depicting the resort's logo "R" in turquoise. Seeing that he had their attention, he gave a slight bow and went on. "*Kachinas* represent different aspects of nature and spirit as well as human life. That particular one provides a blessing to the home."

"I just love your accent," Dottie Faye gushed. "Are you from across the big pond?"

"Yes, indeed, madam." The man smiled and pointed to his gold nametag, which read, "Percival, London, England."

Emma had seen similar nametags at another resort. Including staff's geographic origins was a nice conversation starter, not that Dottie Faye needed any help with that.

"We were in England just last January." Dottie Faye preened. "We stayed with our friend, the Earl of Halsey at Dudley House, his country estate."

"Is that so, madam? I sense you enjoy travel."

"Oh yes, I certainly do. I'm fortunate that my late husband left me quite well-off. The three of us have been doing a lot of traveling in recent months, trying to—"

"That pot is gorgeous," Emma interrupted, pointing to a graceful beige container decorated with faint red stripes and suns. *We don't need Dottie Faye spilling the beans about why we're here.*

Percival moved closer and peered at the pot. "That particular piece is Hohokam Buff Ware, created around 1150 AD. The Hohokam were an early Arizonan tribe." He went on to give them interesting tidbits about the rest of the pottery in the collection. "Everything we have is museum quality," he concluded.

"I'd just love to own some rare pottery," Dottie Faye said with a sigh. "Wouldn't it look good in my living room, Emma Jane?"

Emma thought about Dottie Faye's exuberant Victorian décor with its ruffles, frills, and furbelows adorning furniture, mantel, lampshades, and curtains. "Um, well," she hedged.

"My living room after I redecorate, I mean," Dottie Faye amended. "Simple and modern, that's my new motto."

"Antique pottery is probably terribly expensive," Kelly said. "Thousands, I'd imagine."

"You're right about that," Percival said. "Would you ladies please excuse me? I've got a guest who needs my assistance." He nodded toward a nearby podium marked "Concierge." A man in a polo shirt and shorts stood there, gazing around with an impatient look on his face. "If you have any further needs, please feel free to call on me."

"Oh, we will," Dottie Faye said. "Thank you." She gave him a warm smile and a flutter of her lashes. "Charming man," she said, as Percival walked away. "Maybe he can help me find some pottery. After all, I can afford it."

"Let's not get distracted," Emma said. "We're here to find Dakota Longbone."

"We won't have far to go," Kelly said, nodding toward a poster on an easel nearby. "She's presenting a program on Native American culture here tonight."

Their suite was among the most beautiful hotel accommodations Emma had ever seen. Decorated in subtle earth tones of rich brown, tan, and red ochre, it had a living room, kitchen, three bedrooms, a soaking bathtub in each of the three bathrooms, a deck that overlooked the huge pool, and most spectacular of all, a view of the canyon walls from almost every room.

Emma prepared three glasses of ice water with lemon slices she found in the fridge and brought them out to the deck where Kelly and Dottie Faye were lounging. She handed the glasses around and sat down on a cushioned teak chair. "This place is gorgeous. Thank you so much, Dottie Faye."

"Think nothing of it. Why shouldn't we enjoy ourselves even if we are here on a mission?"

"Speaking of enjoying ourselves, what're you ladies going to do before dinner?" Emma asked. "I need to get some exercise after sitting all day."

Kelly stretched her arms as she yawned. "Exercise? I think I'll take advantage of the sunshine and go down by the pool. You should join me. It's too hot to run right now." She jabbed a thumb toward the thermometer hanging on the wall. Eighty degrees. "I heard the guy at the desk saying it's unusually hot for April."

"You're right. I'll go to the air-conditioned fitness center and work out there. How about you, Dottie Faye?"

"Oh, I don't know," she said vaguely. "I'll probably just rest for a while."

Interesting. Whenever Dottie Faye was vague, there was usually trouble afoot.

A short while later, as Emma huffed and puffed on the treadmill in the well-appointed fitness center overlooking the front entrance, her suspicions were confirmed. Dottie Faye, wearing her cowboy hat and boots but with a skirt and different blouse, emerged from the hotel and got into a large black limousine, assisted by Percival, the concierge. As Emma watched, the black car rolled away, Dottie Faye invisible behind tinted windows.

three

"Another cream cake?" Kelly held the tray out to Emma, who was lounging on a sofa placed at a right angle to the one Kelly sat on. "They're almost as good as the ones we had in England."

After Emma's workout and Kelly's thorough baking by the pool, they had enjoyed luxurious, lengthy showers with the resort's signature soaps, shampoos, and lotions. Then, deciding that they were starving and dinner was too long to wait, they had called room service and ordered high tea. Assorted small sandwiches—smoked salmon, cucumber, and curried egg salad—had been provided along with tiny fruit tarts and cream cakes. Hot English tea with fixings of lemon, cream, and sugar rounded out the meal, along with a small pot of coffee in expectation of Dottie Faye's return. She detested brewed tea.

"No, thanks. I've had enough to eat. But another cup of tea would be great." Emma swung her feet to the floor and sat up, handing her cup to Kelly, who poured the hot liquid. "I'm really getting worried about Dottie Faye. I hope she's not in trouble." Calls to her phone had gone unanswered.

Kelly shrugged off that notion and set the teapot down on the tray. "A day without Dottie Faye's shenanigans is like a day without sunshine." Kelly almost invariably found Dottie Faye's exploits amusing.

"You can laugh, but I'm concerned. That truck hitting us today was no accident."

"Oh, Emma," Kelly scoffed, selecting a raspberry tart. "It was just a drunk driver. Wrong place, wrong time. That's all." She chewed the tart and swallowed. "Besides, no one knows where we are."

"I think we should check and see if your mom told anyone." Emma realized she might be overreacting, but every time they investigated a possible suspect, mysterious things had happened. She remembered the note mailed to the store recently: *"The time for warnings will soon be over! Mind your own business!"* And here they were, tracking down Dakota Longbone.

"All right. If you insist, I'll give her a call. What time is it there?"

"Almost seven-thirty," Emma said glancing at the clock.

"She should be home and finished with dinner." Kelly picked up her phone and called Maeve.

Emma sipped her tea and listened to Kelly's side of the conversation. Maeve apparently gave her a rundown of the store sales for the day. "Mom," Kelly asked, "you haven't told anyone where we are, have you?" From the excited squawking she could hear all the way from her seat, Emma gathered Maeve was vigorously denying it.

Kelly hung up. "Mom hasn't told anyone. In fact, she's been telling people that we're in New York on a buying trip. If they ask, that is. We're away so much that people probably think Mom's the owner."

Emma felt a pang of guilt about her insistence on continuing to look into Rose's death, but she quickly quashed it. She hadn't forced Kelly or Dottie Faye to come along. It wasn't her fault that Rose's former students were scattered around the globe.

Kelly's phone dinged and she glanced at the screen.

"Julie sent me a message on Facebook." She proceeded to read and reply. Then the color drained out of her face as she realized something. "Oh, no. Earlier today Julie posted on her 'Timeline' that we were arriving in Sedona today."

"OK," Emma said. "And that means what?" She used technology out of necessity but was far from expert on the ins and outs of social media.

"It means that all 600 of Julie's friends know where we are."

"And all their friends ...?"

Kelly nodded. "Pretty much. Once something is online, there's no controlling who sees it or where it goes. I've heard of people setting up fake Facebook accounts to access information. And kids often 'friend' a so-called friend of a real friend without realizing that the person isn't who they say they are."

Emma's head was swimming slightly at Kelly's convoluted explanation, but she thought she got it. "So our stalker could pretend to be a college student and weasel his or her way into your information through Julie's account?"

"Exactly. And Julie has so many friends, it'd take weeks to sort through them." Frowning, she quickly typed another message. "I'll tell Julie and Keith not to mention anything more about what we're doing." She set her phone back on the coffee table. "I hate to admit it, but you could be right about that truck."

"I don't want to be right, but we have to face that possibility. Also, if Dakota knows we're here, she might be on the lookout for us. That'll make it difficult to get a DNA sample."

Kelly laughed. "Sounds like a mission for the Dottie-Cams." She was referring to Dottie Faye's concealable video cameras.

"I guess so. I'd hate to miss her talk, though." She gestured to the tourist guides and brochures stacked on the table. "While you were in the shower, I was reading up on the historic

Native American sites near here. There are cliff dwellings and cave paintings I'd love to visit if we have time."

"I can see us now," Kelly joked. "'Very interesting presentation, Miss Longbone. Now may we have a sample of your DNA? Oh, and by the way, you're under arrest.'"

"That would take the fun out of it, for sure."

The main door to the suite rattled open, revealing Dottie Faye, followed by a bellman carrying a large cardboard box in his arms. "Hello, sweet pea and sugar pie," she called out and then instructed the bellman to put the box on the floor between an armchair and the sofa. She gave him a tip, and after he left, she sat down with a sigh. "Anything left in that coffee pot? I'm dry as a bone."

"Where have you been, Dottie Faye?" Emma demanded. "We were worried sick."

Dottie Faye accepted a cup of coffee from Kelly. Looking over the decimated food, she raised one eyebrow. "Not so sick you couldn't stuff yourselves, I see. And good for you, Emma Jane. You're not looking quite so peaked." She peered closely at her niece. "I think you actually got a little color riding in the convertible. Very pretty."

"You didn't answer me, Dottie Faye. I saw you get in that car."

Dottie Faye drained her cup and set it on the coffee table. "I went shopping." She picked up the cardboard box and opened the flaps. "That lovely man, Percival, gave me a lead, and I had to act quickly." She tossed aside paper stuffing and gently pulled a carefully wrapped item from the box. "His friend Fiske took me into town in his limo."

"What did you get, Dottie Faye?" Kelly asked, moving eagerly to the edge of the sofa. "Is it an antique?"

"You'll see." Dottie Faye removed the wrappings to

reveal a bowl with a plain white outside and a black-and-white design of triangles, circles, and wavy lines inside. Its very simplicity was pleasing and held a subtle power.

"It's beautiful," Emma said.

"I love the design," Kelly added.

"Isn't it gorgeous?" Dottie Faye smiled down at the bowl cradled in her hands like a beloved child. "It's a Snowflake piece from the Anasazi tribe."

"Where did you buy it?" Emma asked. A warning note sounded in the back of her mind.

Dottie Faye shrugged. "At a warehouse belonging to a man named Jim Smith. It was a long way from here. On some side road. That's all I know. I didn't really pay attention. I left the driving to Fiske."

Emma held out her hand. "Let me see your receipt."

Dottie Faye pouted. "What's this all about, Emma Jane?"

"Just let me see it, and then I'll tell you."

Dottie Faye handed the bowl to Kelly and dug around in her handbag. She dumped a crumpled piece of paper in Emma's hand. "Here you go."

Emma's half-articulated fear was realized. The so-called receipt was a vague, handwritten scrawl that merely said "pottery bowl" and an amount. An amount so high it made Emma wince. "You paid cash?"

"Yes. They wouldn't take a check. So what?"

Emma picked up the tourist guide and quickly leafed to a certain article. "Dottie Faye, I hate to tell you this, but you may have broken the law. Federal law."

four

"**W**hat on earth are you talking about, Emma Jane?" Dottie Faye protested. "I paid good cash money for my bowl. I didn't do anything wrong."

"You didn't, Dottie Faye, but the seller might have, and it can affect you." Emma proceeded to read the regulations that required any Native American pottery to be sold with documentation about its source and origin. "They're trying to prevent a black market in looted antiquities as well as safeguard against forgeries."

Kelly turned the bowl over and peered at the bottom. "This looks authentic to me. It's not perfect, like a machine-made one would be."

"He told me it was real. Over a thousand years old." Dottie Faye's expression was filled with pain. "I'm not that dumb, y'all. I could spot a fake."

"I'm sure, Dottie Faye, but you still need documentation." Emma jumped up from the sofa and began to pace around. They really didn't need this complication. Clearing her throat, she tried to remain calm. "Do you have Jim Smith's phone number?" She waved the receipt. "It's not on here, and neither is a company name."

"No, I don't. I suppose I could try to find the place again." Her voice trailed off doubtfully.

"Let's call Percival," Emma decided. "He's the one who made the contact, right?" She strode to the side table and picked up the phone, dialed the concierge's desk, and asked for Percival. After a minute, she put the receiver down. "He's gone for the night. We'll have to talk to him tomorrow."

"Too bad you weren't wearing a Dottie Cam," Kelly commented.

"Oh, but I *am* wearing one," Dottie Faye said smugly. She tapped her huge belt buckle. "There's a camera in here."

"Why didn't you say so before?" Emma grumbled. "Let's watch it."

Dottie Faye took off her belt, dug a cord out of her bag, and plugged the camera directly into Emma's smartphone. They watched as a shot of the back of a car seat came to life, bouncing to the sound of an engine. "I started it in the car," Dottie Faye said.

"We can tell," Kelly noted. They watched the seat shift and move as Dottie Faye talked about Southern belles and cowboy hats to Fiske.

They perked up when the car stopped and a concrete walkway, a plain metal door, and the jeans-clad rear of a man came into view. "Is that the driver?" Emma asked. At Dottie Faye's assent, she added, "Maybe we can identify him by his rear view."

Kelly elbowed Emma, suppressing a laugh.

"That camera didn't quite work out the way I hoped," Dottie Faye admitted. "This was just a test run. I didn't know we'd need anything from it."

Dottie Faye and the man entered a narrow hall, and the camera caught a brief view off to the left of a warehouse through another doorway.

"What was in there?" Emma asked.

Dottie Faye shrugged. "I really couldn't tell. Shelves filled with boxes." She made the shape of a cardboard box about two feet square. "Oh, and I saw some pottery urns."

The driver knocked on a door.

"Come in," a voice called.

Inside the office, Dottie Faye shook hands with two men, their midsections and hands the only thing visible.

"No identifying tattoos," Kelly said. "Too bad."

The video camera recorded Dottie Faye and the three men discussing the piece of pottery. The only notable information gathered was that Jim Smith's voice was considerably high-pitched for a man.

"He reminds me of someone," Kelly said. She thought for a minute, then snapped her fingers. "Frank Perdue." At their blank stares, she elaborated. "The chicken man on TV. Perdue Chicken."

Emma snorted. "Everything reminds you of food. Even a squeaky-voiced man."

"Hold on," Dottie Faye said. "He kind of looked like Frank Perdue too." She held up her hand above the floor. "About this tall. Skinny as a fence rail." A pause. "But not as charming as that sweet old chicken man."

"I'd say not," Emma said. "Not if he sold you an illegal piece of pottery." She slumped back in her seat. "I guess we're at a dead end for now."

Dottie Faye's face brightened. "If we can't do anything else right now, I'll just take my precious little antique and put it in my room." She snatched up the bowl. "I'm going to go lie down for a while before dinner. Maybe one of my shows is on TV." Cradling the bowl fondly, she bustled away.

Emma groaned. "Trust Dottie Faye to get us into a jam."

"I heard that," Dottie Faye bellowed from her bedroom. "Don't forget I saved your life today, Emma Jane. If it weren't for my driving skills, we'd all be dead at the bottom of a cliff right about now. Maybe burnt beyond recognition."

"She has a point," Kelly said with a wry smile.

That's Dottie Faye for you. First she'll do something like save your life, then she'll do something else to make you want to kill her. Emma sighed. Hopefully they'd get the provenance of the bowl sorted out, and then they could concentrate on their real goal—the proof of Dakota Longbone's guilt or innocence.

Dinner was in the main dining room, a circular area with a stunning view of the cliffs, which looked close enough to touch.

"This is just gorgeous," Dottie Faye said, tweaking her rose silk sheath as she sat down. The resort required semiformal wear for this venue, so Emma and Kelly were also wearing summer dresses and heeled sandals. The other women were similarly attired, and the men wore ties and jackets. Pleasant classical music played, and lit candles stood on every table.

The waiter handed out menus, and Emma suppressed a gasp. The price of an appetizer was more than she usually spent for a whole meal in a restaurant. "I think I'll just have soup," Kelly said, looking forlorn.

"Nonsense," Dottie Faye boomed. "Eat whatever you like. You need to keep your strength up. Investigations burn a lot of calories."

Guests at the tables around them looked over curiously, making Emma squirm. One man seated alone seemed particularly interested. He looked up from his salad, his eyes meeting Emma's. She quickly looked down at the menu. Was that the man from the plane? It was hard to tell since he wasn't wearing his hat.

Dottie Faye conferred with the waiter about house special-ties, and soon they were indulging in a sumptuous array of gourmet offerings. They split an appetizer of squash blossoms filled with goat cheese. For the main course, Dottie had lamb, Emma had duck breast, and Kelly chose the buffalo tenderloin. Each dish was artistically arranged, and the accompanying potatoes, green beans, kale, and carrots were locally sourced.

"My word," Kelly said, rolling her eyes in ecstasy. "Even I would definitely gain weight if I ate here every day. I can't stop." She chased the final forkful of tenderloin around the plate then snagged a leftover morsel of duck from Emma.

"Someday that metabolism of yours is going to come to a screeching halt," Emma warned. She herself stayed slim with a combination of sensible eating and regular exercise. If she ate like Kelly and gave up jogging .... She shuddered at the thought.

"That day is not now," Kelly said. "Where's that dessert menu?" She eyed a chocolate volcano cake being served at the next table.

Dottie Faye's fork dropped with a clatter, and the other two looked at her in alarm. Was she sick or choking? Fortunately neither. Dottie Faye was smiling and waving her arm vigorously like she was hailing a cab. "It's Buck Rodgers. From the plane."

"Buck Rodgers? Really?" Kelly's eyes were amused.

"Rodgers with a *d*." As the man walked past their table, Dottie Faye called, "Hello again!"

Emma looked up to see the man she'd noticed earlier standing reluctantly beside their table. "Hello, ladies," he said. "Enjoying your dinner?" He was very good-looking, Emma noted, with dark curly hair, hazel eyes, and a chiseled face. His build was muscular and broad-shouldered.

"Oh, yes," Dottie Faye said. "The food is wonderful." She

went on to introduce Emma as "my lovely *single* niece" and Kelly as a "beautiful wife and mother of two." Emma clenched her fists in her lap and gave Buck a smile through gritted teeth. He looked no more comfortable than Emma, and his only response to Dottie Faye's prying questions about his purpose in Sedona was a brief remark that he was there on business.

When he finally escaped, Dottie Faye turned to Emma. "A businessman as well as handsome. You could do worse."

"Maybe he's married."

"No, he isn't. I asked," the irrepressible Dottie Faye said.

"He could be the guy who ran us off the road," Kelly pointed out. "He was at the airport, and now he's here."

Dottie Faye shook her head firmly. "I don't think so. Buck is too much of a gentleman to do something like that. Now let's go get ready for Dakota's talk. Kelly, you can take that dessert with you."

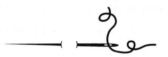

"This wig itches something fierce," Emma whispered to Kelly. They were scurrying down the hall to the meeting room where Dakota was to speak. She pushed her fake eyeglasses back up on her nose. They kept sliding down.

"You think that's bad? I can barely move my face muscles without cracking my makeup." Kelly also wore a wig.

After dinner, they'd expressed to Dottie Faye their fear that Dakota might be watching out for them. Rather than go alone, she'd insisted on disguising them. *At least we'll get to enjoy the talk,* Emma thought, *even if I itch the entire time.*

"Is that blush or leftover chocolate cake?" Emma quipped, reaching out a finger to touch Kelly's cheek.

Kelly ducked away, laughing. "Do you think Dakota will recognize us anyway?" Emma studied Kelly in her blond wig, the glaring lipstick, blush, and eye shadow, as well as one of Dottie Faye's dresses, which hung well past her knees. "Your own husband wouldn't know you." With a sly smile, she pulled out her phone and quickly snapped a photo. "In fact, I'll test it on him."

Kelly screeched. "Oh, you! I don't want anyone to see me this way!" She pulled out her own phone and took a revenge shot of Emma. "You've never looked so lovely, my dear."

"Yes, but who will you send that to?" Emma asked. Dottie Faye's dress was the right length, but it was baggy in strategic places on her.

The two of them burst into giggles, then hurried into the meeting room, managing to grab the last two seats at the back. The lights were dim, but Emma spotted Dottie Faye's massive hair several rows ahead of them. More than fifty people were in the audience, and up front was a projector and screen.

A woman from the resort staff raised her voice to get everyone's attention. "Tonight is the first in a series of lectures and events featuring the history of this region. In addition to learning about the culture, art, and history of our Native American peoples, we'll be exploring cliff dwellings and visiting a working ranch and mining ghost town. You might even see a real ghost or two."

The audience laughed, and Kelly nudged Emma. "That sounds fantastic," she whispered. "Oh, not the ghosts. The rest of it."

The woman went on. "Our speaker and guide this evening is a native of the area and has become one of our local history and art experts. In addition, she's a fiber artist who makes rugs on a traditional Navajo loom. Her work has won awards and is purchased by discerning collectors nationwide. We're lucky to have her with us. Without further ado, a warm welcome for Dakota Longbone."

The audience applauded, and a tall, slender woman with waist-length dark hair moved to the front of the room. As the light hit the planes of her face, Emma saw how beautiful she was, how dignified in her mantle of quiet strength.

Emma felt a pang despite the fact that many murderers were attractive in appearance and manner. *I hope she's innocent.*

Dakota smiled and said in a husky voice, "Good evening, folks, and thank you. I'm so glad to be here. Tonight we're going to do a brief survey of Pueblo arts and discuss one of the spots we'll visit, the Palatki Heritage Site." She turned on the projector and went to the first picture, a map of Arizona and New Mexico. "The Pueblo people still live in the same sites as their ancestors—throughout New Mexico and northern Arizona." A new slide, this one depicting adobe dwellings. "When the Spanish arrived in the 1500s, they found villages of adobe multistory buildings that they called pueblos. They also found a sophisticated social and religious system and a people with advanced skills in pottery, basketry, and weaving."

She went on to show a series of slides showing fine examples of handmade items, including a bowl that was almost identical to Dottie Faye's. "This is an Anasazi Snowflake bowl," Dakota said, "made about 1100 AD." She also informed the group that they needed to verify authenticity before purchasing any items, reinforcing what Emma had told Dottie Faye. Apparently there was a lot of illegal trading of Native American art and antiquities.

I hope Dottie Faye is listening. That bowl is either a black market sale or a fake. Neither is good.

After the presentation, Dakota took a few questions from the audience and then concluded with another invitation for the field trip to the Palaki Heritage Site. This would be an opportunity to see where some of the objects had actually been made a thousand years ago.

"Let's do that," Kelly said, as the lights came back up and the hostess announced that there were refreshments in the hallway.

"I'd love to. Now what should we do?" The rest of the audience was getting up and moving around, chatting and laughing loudly. Dakota was stowing her laptop and cords in a leather tote.

"We can't risk Dakota getting a close look at us," Kelly said. "So we should probably slip out."

"Look. Dottie Faye is going up to talk to her."

As they watched, Dottie Faye made a determined beeline toward Dakota, pushing her way through the crowd. But as she got within speaking distance, Dakota turned and fled, exiting through a side door into another room. Dottie Faye scurried after her, blond hair flying.

five

"What could be taking her so long?" Emma asked, throwing the tourist guide aside. She had memorized almost every attraction in the area while waiting for Dottie Faye to return to the suite. She and Kelly had doffed their disguises and were killing time.

Kelly continued to flip through the television channels, set on mute, staying on each only briefly. She couldn't settle down either. "I vote that if she's not back in ten more minutes, we get dressed again and go looking for her." *Flip. Flip.* "I feel like I did when the kids used to be late getting home. Torn between worry and wanting to wring their necks."

"Dottie Faye seems to have that effect on me lately," Emma said with a hollow laugh. "This is the second time today. I swear I'm going to implant a GPS tracking device in her."

Eight and one-half minutes later, they heard the welcome sound of the door lock rattling. Dottie Faye entered, a smug smile on her face.

"You didn't buy something else, I hope," Emma said, hiding her relief.

Dottie Faye flapped her hand. "No, ma'am." She plopped down in an armchair and slid off her heels. "My dogs are barking tonight." Sensing their impatience, she quickly added, "I got the goods, girls." Digging into her capacious bag, she pulled out a small paper evidence bag. "One cigarette butt. Complete with lipstick stain. I think she wears Clinque Tenderheart."

Emma sagged in relief. "Good job, Dottie Faye. How did you do it?"

"My original plan was to grab her empty water bottle out of the trash, but she took it with her. When I saw how she skedaddled out of that room, I figured she either had to hit the ladies' room real bad or she needed a cigarette. I never smoked, but I do remember when poor Archibald struggled with the habit." She shook her head. "He'd get downright desperate for one. But, of course, I helped him quit." Her smile was wicked. "I won't tell you how."

"And Dakota went out for a cigarette," Kelly prompted.

"Yes. She was out back of the kitchen, by the dumpster. Apparently that's the only place the staff can smoke on the premises."

"What did she think about you chasing her to the smoking area? Didn't she think it was strange?" Emma asked.

"I had to smoke a cigarette too, of course. Or rather, fake-smoke. It's amazing how a fierce need for tobacco fosters new friendships."

"You didn't!" Kelly hooted. "Dottie Faye, you are just too much."

Dottie Faye pulled out a big gold lighter that resembled something Archibald would favor. "You're going to like this even better. I filmed our conversation."

Now Emma joined Kelly in whoops of admiration for Dottie Faye's ingenuity.

"I unpacked my laptop," Kelly said. "Let's plug it in there."

Although it was filmed well after sundown, Dakota happened to be standing under a streetlight near the dumpster, so they could see her clearly. The audio was clear too.

"Hey, that thing produces pretty good quality," Emma said.

"I don't buy junk," Dottie Faye said.

Kelly put up a hand as voices were heard. "Hush. Let's listen."

Dottie Faye introduced herself and made the expected compliments about Dakota's presentation, which she accepted graciously. "Did you grow up around here, Miss Longbone?"

"Please call me Dakota. Yes, I did. I'm a full-blooded Navajo, and I grew up on the reservation north of Flagstaff. I was away for a year or two, but now I'm here to stay."

"It's certainly beautiful country. And I just adore Navajo crafts. Tell me more about your rugs. I'm thinking I might need one."

Dakota laughed. "That's sweet of you. Weaving is my passion, and I spend about every free moment doing it. I was fortunate to learn traditional patterns and methods from my amá sání—my grandmother—before she passed away. The Navajo Nation as a whole is making an effort to pass on our cultural legacy to new generations. Pottery, rugs, and baskets help us do that while providing a living for many of us."

"That reminds me of my niece. She teaches people how to quilt some of the Colonial patterns from the 1600s."

Dakota jerked her head up. "Your niece makes quilts?"

Dottie Faye, realizing her tactical error, tried to change the subject. "Yes, she does, like a lot of people, I suppose. Where can I see your rugs?"

Dakota ignored the question. "I took a quilting class a long time ago. In Mystic Harbor, Massachusetts. I went to Hawthorne College for a year."

The lighter jerked in Dottie Faye's hand, but she didn't emit more than a squeak.

"I transferred back to Arizona State when ... when I lost someone close to me and I needed to be near family."

Dottie Faye patted her arm with a manicured hand. "I understand. I felt the same way when I lost Archibald, my husband." She neglected to mention that his demise had occurred thirty-six years ago, but Emma knew it only seemed like days to her aunt.

"I'm sorry to hear that. My sympathies." Dakota took a drag on her cigarette. "I'm having a show opening tomorrow night at Sedona Originals, a gallery in town. You're welcome to come if you'd like. There'll be a lot of artists' work there, not just mine."

"I'll be there," Dottie Faye promised.

In the background, a metal door slammed and voices came their way, heading for the smoking area.

"Well, I should get going." Dakota dropped her cigarette and ground it out.

Before she could bend over, Dottie Faye dropped her own cigarette. "Don't bother, I've got it." Swooping down, she grabbed both butts and tossed them in the bucket.

"I only threw mine away." Back in their hotel suite, Dottie Faye revealed her sleight of hand to Emma and Kelly.

"Good work, Dottie Faye," Kelly said as she stopped the video program. "That was a close call though, when you mentioned your niece."

"I know. It just slipped out."

"It's hard to tell if she's innocent or not," Emma mused. "If she were guilty you wonder why she'd even mention the class. But then again, she could be trying to throw us off the track."

"That would presuppose she knows someone is on her trail," Kelly pointed out.

"Someone's on ours, that's for sure. The big question is, who?"

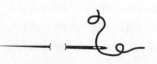

Emma often had trouble sleeping the first night in a new place, and the resort was no exception. In addition, they were three hours behind the East Coast, so six a.m. was really nine in her internal clock, well past her usual rising time. Contributing to her restlessness was an endless churn of thoughts about Rose and the possible futility of their quest. They'd investigated six students so far. If Dakota were innocent, that meant the investigation would have to move to the next one on the list. The very thought was tiring.

Kelly and Dottie Faye didn't seem to be having any trouble sleeping late, so Emma put on her yoga pants and top, left a note, and went to find the sunrise class mentioned in the resort calendar.

The class was held outside on one of the stone-flagged terraces. As the sun's golden rays slipped into the shadowed canyon, Emma stretched and breathed along with two dozen other devotees. The morning air was crisp and cool, perfect for exercising, and fluting birdsong provided a soundtrack to the gentle voice of the instructor. Emma didn't believe in the spiritual vortexes Dottie Faye had mentioned, but she had to admit that the setting had a special beauty and peace. As her breathing slowed, so did the relentless chatter of her thoughts.

Back at the suite, she joined Kelly and Dottie Faye on the deck, where, dressed in the plush white robes provided by the resort, they were eating a hearty but healthy breakfast of scrambled eggs, whole grain toast, fruit, and yogurt.

"There you are," Kelly said. "Want coffee?"

Emma slid into a seat at the table. "You bet. Thanks."

"By your attire, I'm guessing you went to a yoga class," Dottie Faye said. "How was it?"

"Wonderful. This place is really special." Emma served

herself a bowl of yogurt and topped it with blueberries and strawberries. "You both slept well, I take it?"

Dottie Faye stretched. "Oh, yes. I always feel relaxed after completing a mission. I'm going downstairs to overnight that sample to the lab as soon as I get dressed."

"I'm glad I went to Dakota's presentation, despite having to wear a disguise," Kelly said. "Her talk was so interesting. I'm looking forward to that trip to the ruins this afternoon."

"Me too, even if I have to wear that wig again," Emma said. "Until we know Dakota is innocent, I don't want her to know who we really are." Maybe she was being overcautious, but with all the mysterious and dangerous things happening—like being run off the road—she felt more comfortable incognito around their suspect. "Speaking of the talk," Emma said, "I found certain parts of it very interesting. Didn't you, Dottie Faye?" Her gaze at her aunt was pointed.

Dottie Faye fiddled with her robe tie and stared off at the view, which was indeed deserving of notice. "Isn't the play of light on the canyon walls just spectacular? The colors look different as the angle of the sun changes."

"Dottie Faye." Emma's tone was gentle. "You have to give back that bowl. Dakota only reinforced what that article said. It's wrong to hold on to it."

Dottie Faye sighed. "I know you're right. I just love it so."

Kelly put her hand on Dottie Faye's arm. "Don't worry. We'll go to Sedona Originals and find you something else."

"Are you sure this is a good idea?" Kelly asked. With Emma at the wheel of the convertible, they were driving along yet another side road in Sedona. After mailing the DNA sample, they'd gone to the concierge station only to discover that Percival was off for the day. At Emma's insistence, they were trying to find Jim Smith's warehouse anyway, solely from Dottie Faye's memory, which was proving to be faulty. "Those vultures are making me nervous." She pointed at the buzzards circling overhead. "Maybe they know something we don't."

Emma slowed as the pavement ended and the road became red dirt, creased with ruts. "I'm about ready to turn around. We'll just have to give up."

"No, don't," Dottie Faye said. "I recognize that shack over there." She pointed at a tumbledown building, insignificant except for the blooming cactus plants surrounding it. A large, vibrant pink blossom capped each thorny branch.

Kelly sucked in a breath. "I'd heard the desert is beautiful in spring, but I had no idea how spectacular it would be."

Emma had to agree. The flowers had transformed the dull grays and browns of the desert into a pink wonderland.

"The warehouse is just around the next corner," Dottie Faye said.

"Uh-oh," Kelly said. "There's a fence. And a guard."

"You didn't mention a guard, Dottie Faye," Emma said.

Dottie Faye shrugged. "We went right through. It wasn't a problem."

Emma pulled to a stop in front of the gate. A metal fence topped with razor wire stretched in both directions, protecting the cluster of low steel industrial buildings inside. A muscular guard with a shaved head, a surly expression, and a gun strapped to his belt stepped out of the guardhouse.

"Help you?" he barked.

Emma darted a glance at Dottie Faye. "Um, we're here to see Jim Smith. My aunt has business with him."

He gazed at each of them in turn with cold eyes. Emma thought she saw a spark of recognition when he looked at Dottie Faye. "You have an appointment?"

Emma squirmed, wanting more than anything to just turn the car and flee. But she stiffened her resolve. "No, we don't. Can't you call and tell him we need to see him?"

His lips quirked in a nasty smile. "'Fraid not. He doesn't want to be disturbed."

"She wants to return something she bought from him just yesterday," Emma persisted. She tried to hand the receipt to him, but he shook his head.

"No can do." He slapped the car door with his hand. "Go on, get out of here." He stepped back, resting his hand oh so casually on his gun.

Her hands shaking, Emma put the car in reverse, backed, and turned. Then she hit the gas and sped away, heedless of the ruts and potholes jolting the car.

"Whoa, that was scary," Kelly said from the back seat.

"I guess that means I get to keep my bowl," Dottie Faye said with a sigh. "I tried to give it back."

"No, Dottie Faye. It means that something is very, very wrong with that whole operation." Emma's hands tightened on the wheel. No legitimate merchant would refuse to see his customer again. And what kind of pottery business needed a fence and an armed guard anyway? She hesitated to go to the police though. It would be terrible if Dottie Faye got in trouble for an innocent mistake. They'd have to try talking to Percival again, if he ever came back to work.

After a quick lunch in the suite, Emma and Kelly donned wigs, sunglasses, and baseball caps for the tour to the Palatki Ruins. Several vanloads went, and Dottie Faye managed to be included in the lead van with Dakota. Emma and Kelly squeezed into the backseat of another van with a barbershop quartet and their wives.

"They'll be performing later tonight in the lounge," one wife, a plump older woman, told them in her soft Texas twang. "We're all retired, so we travel together several times a year to new locations."

Her white-haired and bearded husband, who reminded Emma of a slender Santa Claus, winked. "The Lone Star Warblers sing for their supper."

His wife elbowed him. "Not quite, Stan. It's all volunteer, with tips going to charity."

"That sounds nice," Emma said politely. "What do you sing?"

"What do we sing?" Stan exclaimed, his furry brows rising in feigned amazement. "Boys, we have a request."

With a "one, two, three," the quartet broke into song, and as the van rolled along dusty dirt roads to their destination, they performed a selection of Western-themed songs, including *Happy Trails*, *Buffalo Gals*, and *Red River Valley*. The wives sang the choruses, and even Emma and Kelly joined in.

"That was great," Emma said as the van pulled into a parking spot near the visitor's center.

Stan's wife patted Emma's arm. "I'm glad you enjoyed it, dear. The boys are a lot of fun." She gazed at Stan fondly, who had leaped out and was now helping the ladies to exit the van. "I'm Bev, by the way."

Emma introduced herself and Kelly, and they scrambled out to join the tour, making sure to stay at the rear of the group of about twenty. Dakota, dressed in khaki cargo pants, a jacket, and hiking boots with a yellow bandanna holding back her inky hair, led them along a dusty, rock-strewn path toward the towering red cliffs. Dottie Faye followed on her heels like a teacher's pet. This close to the rocks, Emma could clearly see the striations that marked eons of sediment deposits. The plant life included sage, juniper, small evergreens, and clumps of prickly pear cacti studded with yellow blossoms along the top of each flat oval pad.

Kelly hunkered down and took a photograph of the bright blossoms. "Don't you think the colors of the cactus flowers would make nice accents to our Southwestern quilts?"

"I was thinking the same thing yesterday when we saw the pink ones."

"People eat those, you know," Bev said. "They're common in Mexican dishes."

"Yuck," Emma said. "How can anyone eat them? They're full of thorns."

"You scrub off the spines." Bev demonstrated with gestures. "Then you slice them up like any vegetable. The young bright green ones, not the old grayish ones." She pointed to the flowers. "Those produce fruit that's used for juice or in recipes."

"Fascinating," Kelly said. "I wonder if it tastes like chicken."

"Studying native plants is one of my hobbies," Bev said. "But if I bore you, please stop me." She continued to give them a mini-lecture as they walked toward the first stop on the tour, appropriately called Red Cliffs.

Emma let Bev's words drift into her mind, absorbing them along with the peaceful beauty of this spot where an ancient people once dwelled. The group stopped under an overhang, and Dakota pointed out white-and-black paintings of animals and figures. There were pictographs and petroglyphs etched into the rock face. "The petroglyphs were made as long as five or six thousand years ago," she said. "The paintings are from about 1100 AD, and were made by people the Spanish called the Sinagua, which means 'without water.' Finding these two types of artwork near each other is very unusual."

"What happened to the Sinagua?" someone asked.

"No one really knows," Dakota said. "Some theories involve drought or competition with other groups coming into the region. For example, the next alcove we're stopping at has Apache and Yavapai pictographs."

After allowing time for everyone to fully examine the art, she led them to the Bear Alcove. As expected, it had paintings of three bears, one large and two small, along with deer and horseback riders.

"I guess Goldilocks is more universal than I thought," Kelly quipped. The people nearby laughed and in response, Dakota glanced their way. Kelly quickly turned her head, feigning interest in another pictograph. Emma crouched and retied her sneakers. Dottie Faye, bless her heart, distracted Dakota with a question about one of the other images. After answering Dottie Faye, Dakota raised her voice and addressed the group. "We have a special treat today," she said. "We're going to see the only known example of an agave roasting pit."

"Agave," Bev said. "Used for sweetener now but also a staple food and medicine. And the blue agave is used to make tequila."

Overhearing Bev, Dakota waved her to the front of the crowd. "Please repeat that for everyone," she said.

Blushing at the attention, Bev explained how ancient people extracted the heart of the agave and roasted it for days underground. She pointed to a nearby spiky plant that resembled a giant aloe vera. "There's an agave plant right over there. And it's getting ready to bloom." Indeed, the plant had a tall spire emerging from its center.

"That's correct," Dakota said. "Native Americans used all parts of the agave. In addition to roasting the heart to eat—much like an artichoke heart—the leaves and juice were used for poultices and medicine. They used the flowers for tea and the seeds for flour. Those were quite a treat as this plant only blooms every ten to twenty years, although people used to think that it was every hundred years, hence another name for *Agave americana* is 'century plant.' The spire will grow as high as thirty feet and produce red flowers later this summer." She called to Emma. "You, in the pink ball cap."

Emma glanced around, hoping Dakota was talking to someone else. She was the only one in a pink cap. "Are you talking to me?"

"Yes. How tall are you?"

"Five feet, eight inches," Emma said.

"What's your name?"

The only thing that popped into Emma's head was "Maeve." She felt Kelly jump and heard her swallow a panicked giggle.

"Well, Maeve, you're the tallest person here, so you get to have your picture taken. Come on up and stand beside the plant. Everyone, take this opportunity to get a picture of a rare botanical event."

Her feet dragging, Emma reluctantly went forward, praying that her black wig, sunglasses, and hat were a sufficient disguise close-up. She cursed her stupidity. She and Kelly could have taken another tour with someone else, she realized belatedly.

Dakota put her hands on her shoulders and moved Emma into position beside the plant. "Don't touch the plant, Maeve. Those black thorns on the edge of the leaves can rip your skin to shreds." Her shiny black eyes were serious as she studied Emma's face. "I've seen the wounds. The sap is poisonous too."

Emma flinched, pulling her leg away from an encroaching spike. Sweat trickled between her shoulder blades. *Does Dakota know who I am? Is she singling me out as a warning?*

SIX

Dakota moved aside, and the group snapped photos of Emma and the plant. She attempted to smile, not wanting to ruin anyone's memory of the trip with her sour face. Then, at someone's suggestion, Dakota stood beside Emma and more pictures were taken. Finally the ordeal was over, and she escaped to Kelly's side, well away from Dakota. She would be so relieved when the lab results came back tomorrow. If Dakota was innocent, then all this subterfuge was for naught. If she was guilty ... Emma shivered to think she might have been standing shoulder to shoulder with Rose's killer.

Emma made sure to stay at the rear of the group for the rest of the tour, which included a visit to the agave burn pit, a wide, dirt-covered area still holding roasted plant hearts from 1864. Apparently, soldiers from Fort Whipple had ambushed the Apaches at the pit before they could eat their feast. Despite her personal turmoil, Emma's heart twisted hearing this sad tale, so emblematic of the West's complex history.

The final stop was at the Sinagua cliff dwelling, built of mud bricks matching the reddish-orange rock surrounding them. Here they were allowed to step inside the rooms of the ancient homes and see the evidence of cooking fires on the soot-stained walls. Bev came up beside Emma while she was standing in one of the rooms contemplating the people who had lived here so many centuries ago and had vanished with so little evidence of their existence. "I always say a little prayer when I'm in a place like this," Bev said quietly. "It's sad that no one remembers the people who lived here. But God does."

I remember you, Rose. I always will.

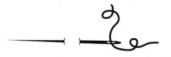

Back at the hotel, Emma and Kelly gratefully took off their wigs, and all three showered and changed.

"What do you want to do now?" Emma asked, joining the others in the living room. "We have a couple of hours before the gallery opening."

"Let's go have a snack at one of the restaurants," Kelly suggested. "If we have dinner after the opening, that's three or four hours from now. I'll starve."

"You two go on ahead," Dottie Faye said. "I'll join you in a bit. I have an appointment for a spirit animal reading."

"A *what*?" Emma exclaimed.

"The Native Americans believe that each person is guided by a spirit animal. A totem. Not that I believe in such things," she added, in answer to Emma's squawk. "It's just for fun."

"Find out what ours are," Kelly suggested, earning a glare from Emma.

"You could come with me," Dottie Faye said. "Your spirit animal is based more on your personality, if I understand it right."

"I don't think we'll be coming along for a 'reading,'" Emma retorted.

"Maybe your spirit animal is a sloth." Dottie Faye left the room in a huff.

Outside the main building's lounge, Emma and Kelly sat on a sofa facing the cliffs. The late afternoon sun tinged the rock formations with gold and created long, dark shadows across the landscape.

"I love this time of day," Emma said.

"Me too." Kelly studied the menu. "How about sharing a tapas platter? We get six different things. Little things," she assured Emma. "Tiny. Not big enough to ruin dinner."

They ordered an assortment of appetizers and a pitcher of iced tea, requesting a third glass and plate for Dottie Faye.

"I almost died when Dakota called you up front," Kelly said. "And I almost died laughing when you called yourself Maeve."

"It was the first name that popped into my head. Maybe because she mentioned my hat. Pink. Mauve. Maeve. Well, they're close."

They stopped talking while the waitress delivered the iced tea.

"I wondered if she did it on purpose," Kelly said, pouring them each a glass. "Did it seem like she knew who you were?"

"I couldn't tell for sure. But she did give me a creepy warning about the agave plant." Emma shuddered. "She told me the thorns could rip up my skin." She added lemon and one sugar to her tea.

"Well, they can," Kelly said. "Did you see how long they were? Scary. Maybe she was just doing her duty as a guide."

"I hope you're right."

Emma and Kelly analyzed their encounter with Dakota until the waitress arrived with a platter of Kobe beef sliders, shrimp wontons, roasted mini-ears of corn, empanadas, cups of macaroni and cheese, and soft pretzels along with a tray of assorted hot, sweet, and spicy sauces.

"Yum," Kelly said eloquently, dabbing barbecue sauce on a slider. "The food here is fabulous."

Emma reached for a pretzel and dipped it in honey

mustard. "You're right," she said after swallowing the savory mouthful. Next she chose an empanada, a triangle of spicy beef and potato. "I'm going to need to take a long run tomorrow."

Kelly snorted. "You're probably wearing off those calories worrying about them."

"Hello, girls." Dottie Faye sank down on the opposite sofa with a sigh. "How's the iced tea?"

Emma poured her a glass. "It's unsweet." Emma had learned from Dottie Faye how Southerners classified their iced tea: sweet and unsweet.

"Thanks for the warning." Dottie Faye picked up three sugar packets and shook them prior to ripping them open and pouring the white crystals into her glass. "I had the most interesting session with the spirit animal reader." She preened. "Guess what I am?" She stirred the tea vigorously.

"I won't even try," Emma said.

"I'm a lioness." She patted her fluffy blond hair as though suggesting it resembled a lion's coat. "My traits are strength, courage, good timing, and strong family ties. Doesn't that sound just like me?"

"Kind of," Emma had to admit.

"What am I?" Kelly asked before tossing a shrimp wonton into her mouth and chewing vigorously while expressing appreciation.

"A pig?" Emma ducked Kelly's flying elbow.

Dottie Faye tasted her tea, made a face, and added three more packets of sugar. "That woman was really good. All I did was describe you girls and she knew right away which animals influence you." She pointed at Kelly. "Fox. Clever, observant, fast, and persistent."

"I'll take that. What about Emma?"

"She's a wolf. They're considered one of the strongest spirit animals." Dottie ticked off the traits. "Steadfast, intelligent, guided by dreams, and able to outwit enemies."

Emma remembered her ongoing dreams about Rose. *How uncanny.* "I don't believe in all that, but at the same time I hope it's right. We've certainly got an enemy to outwit."

"You'll do it, darling. With the help of a lioness and a fox, how can you go wrong?"

Emma pictured the three animals tracking a killer and bit back a smile. Too bad she didn't have a wolf's sense of smell. Maybe then they could sniff him or her out.

"What about Mom?" Kelly asked. "With all the time she is spending watching the shop, she's helping us too."

Dottie Faye waved a dismissive hand. "Oh, Maeve's a donkey. I didn't need a reader to tell me that. Stubborn, won't listen to anybody, always a naysayer." She brightened. "I can't wait to tell her when we get home."

"Mom will be thrilled at hearing she's a donkey," Kelly commented in a sarcastic tone, rolling her eyes. "You better be careful or she might kick you."

"I guess that'd prove my point, wouldn't it?" Smiling with satisfaction, Dottie Faye selected a ramekin of macaroni and cheese from the tray. "Let's see if this tastes as good as my mama's. It's one of the classic Southern side dishes, you know."

"So you've said. Along with greens, corn pudding, fried green tomatoes, and butter beans, to name a few." Emma felt bloated just thinking about the typical Dixie meal of meat and three sides.

Dottie Faye took a taste. "Not bad. We need a good Southern-style restaurant in Mystic Falls—"

A voice behind them interrupted Dottie Faye's rhapsody about the merits of her native dishes.

"Emma? Emma Cotton? Is that you?"

Emma turned her head to see the one person she had been hiding her identity from for the last two days. The one who'd made her suffer with itchy wigs and unflattering disguises in pursuit of that apparently fruitless attempt. Dakota Longbone.

"Busted," Kelly whispered.

seven

Emma stared at Dakota, not sure what to say or do. "Yes, I'm Emma Cotton," she finally croaked. Equally confounded, Kelly and Dottie Faye looked on with wide eyes.

"I thought so!" Dakota crowed. Taking Emma's shock for confusion, she added, "I'm sorry. Of course you don't remember me. It was years ago when we met." She perched on an armchair, arranging the long full skirt she wore with cowboy boots and a Western shirt. "It was when I was a student at Hawthorne. You were having lunch in the cafeteria with my textiles instructor, Rose Peterson. You remember Rose, right?"

Do I ever. If only I knew if Dakota is as innocent as she seems. Or maybe she's a fox playing a cunning game. "Rose was one of my good friends," Emma said. "We often ate lunch together."

"I remember you were interested in textiles too," she said. "Did you ever do anything with that?"

"Oh, yes. I own a quilt design shop in Mystic Falls called Cotton & Grace. This is my partner." Emma introduced Kelly and Dottie Faye, pretending she didn't know Dottie Faye had been pestering Dakota since they arrived.

"I've had the pleasure of meeting Mrs. Sinclair," Dakota said, gazing back and forth between Emma and her aunt. "She was on my tour today. And at my lecture last night."

"Yeah, I was sorry to miss that," Emma said, a hot blush suffusing her neck. "We just got here." It took a lot of effort and nerve to keep up the subterfuge. She'd never make a good undercover investigator. Right now she was suppressing an impulse to throw herself on Dakota's impeccable shirtfront and blurt out everything. "But we're planning on coming to your art show opening tonight," she said to change the subject.

Dakota beamed. "Really? I'd love that. I'm doing rugs now, but I certainly learned a lot from Rose. She actually helped me discover an appreciation for the design genius of my ancestors' work."

"They were geniuses," Kelly put in. "Such a sense of color and design. Simple but powerful. Even today—" She broke off, realizing that she supposedly hadn't seen the cave paintings that afternoon either. She swallowed. "I was looking at Dottie Faye's handouts from your presentation, and wow! I was really impressed."

Good save, Kelly. "The colors and shapes of this gorgeous landscape are inspiring all kinds of project ideas," Emma added, with a gesture at the cliffs, "We're going to do a Southwest series."

"That'll be wonderful," Dakota said. She glanced at her watch then jumped up. "I've got to get to the gallery to get ready for the show, but it was so nice running into you. See you tonight!" With a swing of her long, shiny hair, she was gone, weaving through tables and chairs toward the patio door.

Emma sank back in her seat. "Oh, my. I thought I was going to have a heart attack when she called my name."

"She was either genuinely surprised or the most devious person I've ever met," Kelly said.

"My money is on her innocence," Dottie Faye said. "She's a sweet girl."

"I'm not going to bet against you, Dottie Faye," Emma said dryly. "I can't afford it. I hope those results come in soon so we know the truth about her, that's all."

"Amen to that," Kelly said. "Anyone want the last shrimp wonton? No? Then I'll make the grand sacrifice of eating it."

With Dottie Faye at the wheel of the convertible, they drove into downtown Sedona. All three wore pretty summer dresses and shawls around their shoulders to ward off the cool night air. Emma and Kelly let the breeze ruffle their hair, thankful they no longer had to hide under wigs.

The Sedona Originals gallery was on the main street next to Hacienda Grill, a lively restaurant with umbrella-covered tables on the sidewalk. Dottie Faye found a parking space up the block, and they walked back, high heels clicking on the sidewalk, enjoying the festive atmosphere of the classic Western-style downtown. The sun was rapidly setting now, and the first stars emerged in the indigo blue sky above, joined by a slice of moon.

"Let's have dinner there," Dottie Faye said, pointing to the grill. "It must be good if it's so crowded."

"I'm sure the art show is drawing people too," Emma said as they waited behind a foursome of well-groomed older people entering the gallery. The wide plate glass windows on both sides of the door displayed a selection of rugs, pottery, baskets, and jewelry arranged attractively under warm amber lighting.

"I'll make us a reservation," Kelly offered. "How about an hour from now?"

"Good idea," Emma said. "We'll meet you inside."

The gallery was larger than it appeared from outside, a long narrow space holding numerous display alcoves set off

by walls or cases. Near the front cashier's area, tables held
wine, beer, and water next to vegetable and cheese plates.
Attendees milled about looking at exhibits, chattering, and
enjoying refreshments.

"How nice Dakota has a big turnout," Dottie Faye said.
"Would you be a love and get me an ice water?"

Emma pushed through the crowd and secured drinks. By
then Kelly was back, so they began to work their way through
the gallery looking at the artwork and hoping to find Dakota.
The first section had handcrafted jewelry displayed in cases,
much of it silver and turquoise. On top of the cases was
information about the artisans who had created the pieces.

"Oh, how gorgeous," Emma said, pointing to delicate
silver bangles inlaid with slivers of pale turquoise. "They're
so dainty."

"I love them too," Kelly said, joining Emma at the case.
Then she gasped. "Wow, they're a little bit out of my budget."

"Probably everything is in here," Emma agreed. "But
it's fun to look." Whirling around, she bumped into a tall,
handsome blond man dressed in a very expensive suit. He
grabbed her elbow to steady her.

Spotting a good-looking man in proximity to Emma,
Dottie Faye fluttered over from the earring display she'd
been examining.

"Pardon me," he said, gray eyes twinkling. He dropped
Emma's arm. "I'm Marc Jacoby, the gallery owner. Are you
enjoying the show?"

Emma squeezed by him, not comfortable with someone
invading her personal space. "So far. We just got here."

Seeing that Emma was trying to avoid Marc's overtures,
Dottie Faye stepped in and made introductions. "Can you tell
us where we can find Dakota Longbone's work?" she asked,

batting her eyelashes. "I'm very interested in adding a Navajo rug to my collection."

Marc tore his eyes from Emma's face. "I'd be happy to show you, Mrs. Sinclair. Right this way."

With a well-placed elbow or two, Dottie Faye maneuvered things so Emma was beside Marc as he led them through the gallery. "So, Emma, are you enjoying Sedona?" he asked.

"Yes," Emma said.

Dottie Faye piped up. "We loved the Palatki Ruins, didn't we, dear?"

"They were fantastic," Emma agreed. "Especially the pictographs."

"If you enjoyed those, I'd be happy to take you to some other sites," Marc offered. "I know some secret places most tourists never see."

"Ooo!" Dottie Faye exclaimed with a clap of her hands. "What a lovely offer. You'd like that, wouldn't you, Emma?"

Emma was saved from having to answer by their arrival at the rug display. She stopped short, overwhelmed by the sheer beauty of the dozen or so pieces hanging on the walls. They featured several designs—two diamonds, stripes, arrows, triangles, and Xs—and all had unifying shades of desert-inspired colors. The artful hanging sequence created an emotional impact akin to gazing at the sweeping grandeur of Sedona's cliffs and rock formations.

Kelly read from the artist's statement posted on the wall: "Instead of focusing on a single traditional design from her region, as is common, Dakota Longbone has used several designs in a thematic display interpreting the beauty of the desert landscape. In preparing her yarns, she incorporated heritage plant dyes, including sunflower, sagebrush, juniper, Indian paintbrush, onion skins, and snakeweed."

Dakota appeared quietly at their side. "So what do you think?" she asked.

Marc, apparently seeing that he had lost Emma's rather marginal attention, melted away with a murmur about seeing to other guests.

Emma stood riveted, hands clasped, her gaze skipping from rug to rug. "As one textile artist to another, I salute you," she said warmly. "I love how you've taken traditional designs and methods to make something uniquely yours."

Dakota ducked her head, and a blush suffused her tanned cheeks. "Thank you for that."

Dottie Faye put her hand on Dakota's arm. "Is Marc Jacoby single?"

Dakota blinked at Dottie Faye, clearly unsure how to answer tactfully, since Marc looked to be about thirty-five or forty, much younger than Dottie Faye.

"Not for me, of course," Dottie Faye said, picking up on Dakota's thought. "He seemed interested in Emma, that's all."

"Dottie Faye! Cut it out," Emma protested. She turned to Dakota. "She's always trying to play matchmaker."

"Really? That's sweet. And yes, he is single." A frown flashed across her face. "But—" Dakota's remark was interrupted by an older woman wearing significant diamond jewelry who absolutely demanded her attention that moment. Another wave of gallery-goers crammed into the display area, further separating them from Dakota.

"I wonder what she was going to say," Kelly said.

"Maybe she's dating him," Emma said.

"But he practically asked you out."

Emma shrugged. "So what? Forget Marc, and let's take a closer look at the rugs. That's why we're here, not to find me a husband. Right, Dottie Faye?

Dottie Faye ignored that. "I just want all of them," she said. "Help me pick one."

Emma sincerely hoped Dottie Faye wasn't supporting Rose's murderer with her purchase, but she tried to put that aside and help her choose the perfect rug. The final selection was one with a two-diamond design, a bold pattern that suited Dottie Faye's personality. Emma was glad to hear Dottie Faye asking Marc's assistant for a receipt as he placed a red dot on the wall beside the rug, denoting that the piece was sold.

"It's about time for dinner," Kelly said, looking at her watch.

"Just let me go to the ladies' room, and we can leave," Emma said. The assistant pointed the way, and Emma found the restroom down a hallway at the back of the gallery, past several closed doors she assumed were offices and storerooms. While she waited in line for the small facility, she saw Dakota slip down the hall and disappear into one of the rooms. Her face looked angry, and Emma wondered if she had been right about Marc and Dakota's relationship.

A few minutes later, after finally accessing the bathroom, Emma hurried back up the hallway. Kelly and Dottie Faye were probably having fits waiting for her. The door to the room Dakota had entered was ajar and as she went by, her attention was caught by loud voices. Despite herself, she slowed to listen.

"The truth about the murder is going to come out," Dakota said, sounding on the verge of tears. "It has to, right?"

Emma halted. Was Dakota talking about Rose?

"There's no evidence," Marc replied. "Otherwise they would have made an arrest already."

"You never know. They might be building a case." Emma heard sniffing and nose blowing along with approaching footsteps. "I'd better get back out there. Mrs. Thatcher wants to buy one of my rugs. At least the show is going well."

Emma bolted down the hall, hoping she made it around the corner into the gallery before Dakota spotted her and figured out she'd been listening.

Footsteps sounded behind her and she risked a glance back. Buck Rodgers, the man she'd seen on the plane and at the resort, was striding down the hall. What was he doing here? Was he an innocent gallery-goer, or had he been with Marc and Dakota?

"I can't believe you bought me this bracelet, Dottie Faye," Emma said, turning her wrist to admire the silver and turquoise bangle in the soft amber light hanging over their booth in the Hacienda Grill. The busy restaurant resounded with laughter, the clatter of dishes, and savory odors of mesquite-smoked meat drifting from the open-air kitchen.

Dottie Faye shrugged and took a bite of her side salad. "What's money for if you can't spend it on those you love?"

"I guess you love me too, then," Kelly quipped, admiring her matching bracelet.

"I do, sweet pea, I do." Dottie Faye pushed her plate aside as the server, a slim young man named Willem, brought their main dishes. She and Kelly had ordered grilled chicken with sides of garlic mashed potatoes and roasted broccoli. Emma had a salad bowl with mixed greens, goat cheese, walnuts, and dried cranberries.

For a few minutes everyone dug in, Emma finding herself surprisingly hungry even after eating appetizers a couple of hours ago. It'd been a long day. They'd explored back roads trying to return the bowl, gone on the ruins tour, and attended a gallery opening. That was a lot.

As though reading her mind, Kelly yawned. "I'm pooped. And gosh, I hope we get the DNA test back tomorrow. The suspense is killing me."

"Me too," Emma agreed. "I wonder if Dakota was referring to Rose when she was talking to Marc." She had told the other two what she overhead when they first arrived at the restaurant.

"Whether she was talking about Rose or another murder, I don't want you dating him, Emma Jane," Dottie Faye said.

Emma snorted. "There wasn't a chance of that. Please stop trying to set me up everywhere we go."

"Dr. Eric is a better match anyway." Dottie Faye's smile was smug. "I hope we figure out this DNA thing too, so I can get on with enjoying our vacation. I still haven't had a chance to go to those cute clothing boutiques. And there are a lot of other sights to see."

Emma and Kelly concentrated on their dinners while Dottie Faye rambled on about the recommendations she'd gotten from everyone she'd met. "They say the sunrise is just magical. Of course I'll never see it because I always make sure I get my beauty rest. How else do you suppose I've stayed so young-looking?"

This last line was delivered to the waiter, who came by to refill their water glasses. He gave her a startled, "Yes, ma'am, you are, uh, youthful indeed." He fled.

"I'm going to give that boy a big tip," Dottie Faye said.

Emma studied her kind and generous aunt, so lovable with all her quirks and foibles. With a jolt she thought of the Snowflake bowl again. They just had to get rid of it, or Dottie

Faye could be in serious trouble. She shuddered at the idea of her aunt in legal hot water.

Back at the suite, Kelly and Dottie Faye went right to bed, but Emma found herself wide awake. The pending truth about Dakota and the ongoing problem of the illicit bowl weighed heavily on her mind, tensing her overfull tummy with uncomfortable worry. She brewed a cup of herbal tea in hopes that it would be relaxing and flopped down on the sofa to watch a little television. Maybe something boring and sleep-inducing would be on. She flicked past the weather channel, a baseball game, an old movie, and a snapshot of a handsome, smiling Native American man with the caption, "John Longbone." She quickly switched back to that channel.

John Longbone? Was he related to Dakota?

"Police have no new information regarding the murder of John Longbone, found dead in his home last week. Longbone, who was co-owner of Sedona Originals, was the victim of an apparent robbery."

Sedona Originals. Then he had to know Dakota.

Emma's thoughts alternated between sympathy for Dakota's possible loss and the unfortunate coincidence of her connection to two victims. But, of course, the motivations and methods were entirely different. Or were they? They hadn't said how Longbone died. If he was pushed ....

"Longbone's death was determined to be a gunshot wound from a small caliber gun. Police have not found the weapon."

Different murder methods then.

Longbone's photograph was replaced by a shot of a black-and-white pottery bowl.

That looks just like Dottie Faye's bowl.

Dread trickled through Emma's veins. She pushed the tea aside, unable to stomach it further.

"Police have not located this Anasazi bowl, with an estimated value of $15,000," the newscaster said.

Emma gulped. If that was Dottie Faye's bowl, it was indeed extremely valuable. And stolen.

"The rare piece was taken from Longbone's home along with other artifacts and cash from a safe. Anyone with information regarding the murder or stolen items should contact the police—"

Emma lay back against the couch and covered her face with her hands. Now she knew Dottie Faye was in big trouble.

eight

Naturally, Emma couldn't sleep, even after she took another hot shower and put on her softest jammies. She lay in bed staring at the ceiling, turning from one side to another, trying and abandoning all the usual tricks. Counting sheep. Counting backward. Practicing the deep breathing techniques she'd learned at yoga. When she did lapse into a doze, she was startled awake by bad dreams about Rose and John Longbone featuring guns and blood and treacherous staircases.

At one point, while lying on her side facing the balcony door, she heard something rattle. It was too dark to really see anything at all; the glowing letters of the clock radio reading three o'clock were the only illumination. There it was again. A rattle like a door handle being turned and the door itself being pushed.

Heart pounding, Emma slipped out of bed and crept to the door. She had double-checked the lock, so she wasn't afraid anyone could actually come in. But if a prowler was lurking, she wanted to find out who it was. A shade was pulled over the door, so she approached it from the side and tried to peer through the edge that hung away from the glass.

Nothing. No movement, no shadowy figure trying to look in. She considered opening the door to see if someone was on the deck but decided that was a bad idea. Why make it easier for a burglar—or worse—to get into the suite? She would definitely report the incident to the manager in the morning. A resort this expensive and exclusive should have better security.

With that disgruntled thought, she threw herself back into bed. She had better get some rest, or she would feel terrible in the morning.

When the gray light of dawn crept into the room, she gave up on sleeping any longer. She might as well celebrate Sedona's famous sunrises with an early morning run. It had been a couple of days since she'd been running, and she was aching to get out there to stretch her legs and burn off some nervous energy. The big round thermometer on the deck read 40 degrees, so she pulled on a long-sleeved T-shirt and light jacket over her sports bra and running shorts. She could take the jacket off once she warmed up. Socks and sneakers were next, and once she put her hair into a ponytail, she was ready to go. To find a route, she checked the resort map in the services guide. The three-mile trail with a mix of hills and level ground leading through the canyon sounded perfect.

She had her hand on the doorknob when she considered the probable reaction of Dottie Faye and Kelly if they woke up to find her gone. Using a piece of resort stationery and a pen, she wrote them a quick note, including the time and her route. But by the sound of Dottie Faye's snores, she would probably be back well before they rolled out of bed.

For a split second, she considered waking them so they could share the sunrise, smiling at the thought of their shrieks and screams of anger and the flying pillows sent her way. Shaking her head at her own mischievous idea, she left the suite.

The trail began by the swimming pool, deserted at this hour, and wound among sagebrush and flowering cacti toward the cliffs, flaming an even brighter red and orange with the sunrise. It was a perfect time to run; the air was fresh and cool. Birds twittered and sang as they greeted the new day.

What a wonderful way to experience the desert—moving alone through nature, absorbing the sights, smells, and sounds.

She had entered an area hemmed in by boulders and cliffs on both sides when an uneasy feeling prickled the back of her neck. Maybe she wasn't alone out here, although she had yet to see another runner or walker. She glanced up at the rock face, seeking a sign of movement or a glimpse of someone watching her from the shadows. She thought of the times she had told other women to listen to their instincts, not to discount apprehensive feelings about people or situations.

It could be the prowler. Maybe he followed me out here.

A deep instinctive part of her kicked in, lending wings to her feet. Adrenaline surging through her limbs, her pulse racing, she sped around a sharp corner, thinking perhaps she could hide somewhere until she was sure no one was following.

She almost stepped on a rattlesnake, its fat, gray-brown coils camouflaged by the matching colors of the desert landscape. The deadly serpent lay on a flat rock warmed by a shaft of sunlight right in the middle of the path. The same instincts that spurred her speed now halted her almost before she had time to process the sight.

She shrieked in fear, jumping backwards.

The snake raised its head and rattled its tail in warning, tongue flicking as it uncoiled. Emma stood frozen, obviously unable to run past the snake blocking her path. But before she could turn and flee, she heard footsteps pounding down the trail behind her. Emma was trapped, caught between a snake and a hard place. She shot a quick prayer heavenward.

Help me.

She took a couple of careful, cautious steps backward. The snake's head continued to bob and weave. Hadn't she read that you should back away slowly and not startle the snake?

She wished she knew how quickly and how far they could move when striking.

The pounding footsteps drew closer, but she didn't dare to take her eyes off the snake to see who was coming. She prayed it was just another jogger. Preferably someone who knew how to handle snakes.

"Whoa. That's a diamondback," a deep voice said. "Their venom is *muy malo.*"

She turned her head to see Buck Rodgers. Again? He seemed to turn up everywhere. Was he following them? Could he be the pickup driver or the prowler?

"What are you doing here?" she demanded, her fear momentarily overcome by annoyance.

He shrugged, not moving his eyes from the snake. "What's it look like?" He, too, wore shorts, sneakers, and a T-shirt, rings of sweat staining his underarms. "Don't get any closer to that rattler."

"I wasn't planning on it, believe me. I almost stepped on it."

He gave a rueful grin. "That must've been exciting."

"A little too exciting for me," Emma replied tartly. "I guess we should go back the way we came."

He shook his head. "We can get by. Follow me."

Not entirely convinced that she should, Emma found herself shadowing Buck as he led the way up and over a slight rise bordering the trail, well out of reach of the snake. With relief, she saw it slither off into the rocks in the opposite direction. Now it wouldn't threaten anyone else.

"You're all set," Buck said, once they climbed back down onto the trail. "Keep going on this loop. It'll bring you back to the resort. I'm going up that hill trail." He pointed to a branch leading steeply off the main route.

Despite her suspicions, Emma was oddly reluctant to part ways with Buck. "Thanks for rescuing a damsel in distress," she said. She still felt the shock of coming across the deadly creature and hoped she wouldn't see others on the trail. But it would be worse if she didn't see them, of course, just felt their venomous fangs in her ankle.

"Do you want me to follow you back in case you run into any more wildlife?" he asked, obviously picking up on her trepidation.

"I hate for you to change your plans." The fact that he had planned a route different than hers meant he was harmless, right? She hoped.

"Don't worry about it," Buck said. "Go on. I'll bring up the rear."

Emma started off, her pace improving once she loosened up again. Buck kept his distance. They ran deeper into the canyon where the sunlight hadn't yet penetrated, and despite the coolness of the air, Emma was relieved. Snakes liked warmth and sun. She had mixed feelings about her companion. Right now she appreciated having him just in case, but it was really odd that he kept turning up wherever she went.

With relief, she saw that they had reached the end of the loop, which emerged in a different part of the resort, near the tennis courts. With a wave goodbye, Buck jogged down one of the cement walkways, headed to his room, she guessed.

He's probably staying here. No big mystery as to why he was on the trail. Just another early morning jogger.

Emma walked to cool down, her pace slowing along with her breathing and heart rate. Then she looked around, trying to get her bearings, and located the main building a distance away. On her way back to the suite, an unusual edifice caught her eye. Made of red stucco, it looked like it was built right into the rock face, with curving walls and a couple of small round windows resembling portholes.

What could it be used for?

As she drew closer, she saw a metal sign with gold letters that read Celestial Grotto set among a bed of poppies, larkspur, and daisies. She laughed. Dottie Faye would love it. Maybe it was the portal for one of those vortex things.

"Beam me up, Scotty," she muttered, staring at the building.

"Aye, aye, cap'n."

Emma whirled around to see Dakota striding toward her. Today she wore tan jeans and a jean jacket with a coral-and-silver beaded T-shirt underneath. Matching coral jewelry ornamented her ears, wrists, and neck, contrasting nicely with the dark gleam of her loose hair.

"Good morning, Emma. You're up and about early."

"I just got back from a run. What are you up to?"

Dakota pointed at the grotto building. "I'm going to morning meditation. You should come too." Emma was doubtful. "Don't worry," Dakota said, "it's not one of those fringe, New-Age things. A chaplain leads it."

Emma tugged on her shorts. "I'm not exactly dressed for it."

"Don't worry about it. Everything here at the resort is pretty casual. I'm going down to the gallery after this, or I'd be wearing shorts myself."

Despite her misgivings, Emma was curious about the strange building. It didn't disappoint. After following Dakota through a small foyer, she entered the main room, a round, domed, rough-hewn expanse supported by thick brown beams. Sunlight streamed through an opening in the center, illuminating murals of Native American life on the tan stucco walls. Here and there rock crystals set into the clay sparkled and glimmered. Dakota led her to a spot on the wooden bench circling the room, between a thirtyish African-American couple in tennis togs and an Asian family. Bev and her husband, Stan from the barbershop quartet, were seated across the way, and she gave Emma a little smile and wave.

Emma sat back against the cool, textured wall and gazed at the sunlight's play on the crystals. She recognized pale purple amethyst, white and rose quartz, and gorgeous deep blue azurite. Gentle yet soaring pipe music with the natural elements of birdsong and running water played from hidden speakers, adding to the atmosphere of peace. No outside sound penetrated the thick walls, giving the place the feel of a cave deep in the cliffs. Perhaps this was how the Anasazi buildings at the Palatki Ruins felt when they were whole, centuries ago.

Beside her, Dakota seemed oblivious to the room's charms. She sat with her head bent, fingering a strand of topaz beads. *Prayer beads?* Emma wondered again if the murdered John Longbone was related to Dakota. That would explain her solemn, prayerful demeanor. *But were Dakota and Marc talking about John Longbone's death the night of the show, or was the conversation about Rose's murder?*

The music stopped, and a Native American man entered the room, dressed in white shirt, white pants, and a clerical collar. A brightly embroidered stole gave his outfit a cheerful air. "Welcome to morning meditation," he said, smiling around at the group. "I'm Chaplain Brian. For those of you used to traditional church services, I apologize. This is more of an opportunity to quiet oneself with a few relaxing stretches followed by visualization or prayer." He gestured. "Up, up," and everyone stood, Emma with a suppressed roll of the eyes.

But the Sun Salutation postures and breathing exercises

were familiar, movements she'd often made in yoga class. As always, it felt wonderful to limber up and allow all thoughts and tension to drain away. After the chaplain felt they were all sufficiently warmed up, he shared a Navajo prayer. "It was learned at my grandmother's knee." His deep voice was resonant as he recited:

"In harmony may I walk.
With harmony before me may I walk.
With harmony behind me may I walk.
With harmony above me may I walk.
With harmony underneath my feet may I walk.
With harmony all around me may I walk.
It is done in harmony."

Emma allowed the words to sink in, and then she said a short prayer of her own, once again asking God to help her find Rose's killer and bring him or her to justice. She asked for wisdom, guidance, and protection for herself, Kelly, and Dottie Faye on their quest.

After finishing the prayer, the chaplain found a seat on the bench and lowered his head in his own thoughts and prayers. The music started again, and a pleasant scent of sage and sweetgrass drifted through the building. Emma felt a surge of peace, a sense that her prayers were heard. She allowed herself to savor it, knowing that the press of circumstances often conspired to rob her of that sweet restfulness.

We are guided step by step, she reflected. Her personal challenge came in believing that all would work out, even if she relaxed her relentless focus for a minute and dared to loosen her grip on the helm of events. *Remember, we don't walk alone.*

Hearing a muffled sound beside her, she opened her eyes to see Dakota bent over even further, shoulders shaking.

She was crying.

nine

Almost without thinking, Emma put her arm around Dakota's shoulders. "Is this about John?" she whispered. Dakota nodded. Around them, people got up and moved toward the door, the service having ended. The chaplain headed in their direction, but Emma warded him off with a headshake and slight smile.

Once everyone was gone, Dakota raised her head and wiped her eyes. "Sorry about that," she said. "I didn't mean to have a public meltdown."

Emma dropped her arm, giving Dakota a pat on the shoulder. "Don't worry about it. I know how it is to lose someone you love."

Dakota's reddened, puffy eyes studied Emma's face. "You do know, don't you? John was my cousin and one of my best friends since childhood."

"I lost my best friend too," Emma said. "Listen, why don't you join Dottie Faye, Kelly, and me for breakfast?"

Dakota looked at her watch. "I have a little time before I have to be at the gallery, so I'd love to. If you're sure it's no imposition."

"No, of course not. We'd be glad to have the company." She stood up and stretched, then rubbed her behind. "That bench was kind of hard."

Dakota got to her feet with a groan of agreement. "How did you know about John?"

"I heard about his death on the news last night and

thought he might be related to you. What a horrible thing to happen."

Dakota nodded grimly. "It certainly is."

Feeling her phone buzz in her back pocket, Emma dug it out and checked for messages. She'd forgotten she had it, or she would have let her friends know she was going to be longer than expected. "Where are you?" Kelly wrote. "Breakfast by pool."

Emma quickly texted back, arranging for Dakota to join them while she ran back to the suite and showered. She threw on a flowing floral cotton sundress and sandals, slathered on sunscreen, and hurried down to the pool.

As she approached the trio sitting under an umbrella in a prime spot next to exuberantly flowering and fragrant bushes, Dottie Faye lifted a slender glass filled with orange juice. "I've got news, sweet pea. The medical test came back negative." She wore a Western shirt and a full, flowing skirt in pale blue, her hair in a flowing, country-singer style.

Emma pulled back a chair between Kelly and Dakota and sat, not sure exactly what Dottie Faye was referring to. With Kelly's wink it sank in. "Oh, that is good news." The DNA test must have come back. Dakota was innocent. Of course that meant they hadn't found the killer, but by the smiles on the others' faces, she knew they were glad that Dakota wasn't the one. "That was quick," she said.

"They have a super-duper express priority service now," Dottie Faye said smugly.

"I'm glad everything's OK," Dakota said with obvious sincerity.

"So are we," Emma said, reaching for the pitcher of juice.

"That's mimosas," Kelly warned. "Champagne and orange juice."

Emma pulled her hand back. "Oh. I'd like just regular juice." She glanced around for the server. "Did you order breakfast yet?"

"No," Kelly said. "We were waiting for you." She picked up a mug. "I'm surviving on coffee. Good thing it has cream. I need the sustenance."

"You didn't have to," Emma said, "but thanks. It's nice to have breakfast together." She looked around for the server, who noticed her and bustled over to take their orders. Kelly had Belgian waffles and sausage; Dottie Faye the yogurt and a fruit bowl with wheat toast; Emma scrambled eggs with cheese and an English muffin; and Dakota a mini-bagel with berries and cream cheese. "This is my second breakfast," she explained, "so I can't fit much more in."

While waiting for their food, they idly discussed what to do with their day. Both Kelly and Dottie Faye seemed relieved about the DNA tests and ready to enjoy their vacation, but Emma hadn't forgotten the Snowflake bowl. She decided to wait until after Dakota left to bring it up.

Dottie Faye waved an orange flyer and almost hit the server, who was carrying a tray holding the breakfast orders. "I found this flyer of metaphysical workshops in the hallway. That spirit animal thing was so much fun, I'm thinking about learning how to read auras or use crystals for healing." She leaned back to let the server place the bowls of yogurt and toppings in front of her.

"Aunt Dottie!" Emma used the "Aunt" part—which Dottie Faye hated—when she was going too far. She needed strength to deal with her aunt.

Dottie Faye ignored her and squinted at Dakota. "Let me guess. Your spirit animal is a panther. You're intuitive and artistic with a hidden fierceness."

Laughing, Dakota spread cream cheese on a bagel half and adorned it with blueberries. "Thanks. I'll take that description. You seem like a natural at reading people."

"Oh, I am," Dottie Faye bragged. "I helped the woman do the reading for Emma and Kelly. And Maeve. She's Kelly's mother. Guess what she is? A donkey." Snorting with glee, she added fruit to her bowl of yogurt and sprinkled granola on top.

"Donkeys aren't all bad," Dakota said. "They're often highly intelligent."

"Mom is smart," Kelly put in. She took a bite of Belgian waffle smothered with melting butter and syrup and quickly chewed.

"Maybe some donkeys are," Dottie Faye muttered with a scowl.

Emma changed the subject entirely, throwing an idea out like a lasso reining Dottie Faye in. "I have an idea. Let's go shopping. I would love to get a T-shirt like Dakota's. Where did you get it?" she asked.

Dottie Faye's eyes brightened at the thought of shopping. Emma really didn't care for it and often resisted her aunt's tireless attempts drag her into stores.

Dakota glanced down at her pretty shirt. "At the boutique next to the gallery. They have lots of nice things. I go there all the time."

"If we go shopping later, I'll forget all about those silly classes," Dottie Faye said, almost bribing Emma.

"That sounds great," Emma said quickly. "I can't wait."

"I'm in," Kelly said. She gestured at her shorts and tank top. "I'm in the mood for something pretty to wear."

The server came to collect their empty plates. "Do you need anything else?" she asked.

"A round of coffee refills, please," Emma said. "Dakota,

if you have a few more minutes, Kelly and I have something to discuss with you."

She shrugged. "Sure."

After the woman brought the steaming carafe over and topped off their mugs, Emma took a deep breath and began. "Remember Rose Peterson? Your visual design instructor?"

"Yes, of course," Dakota said. "She was wonderful. Her class helped me so much with designing my rugs."

"Kelly and I have been investigating her death."

Dakota looked puzzled. "I heard that she accidentally fell down the stairs at school." She shuddered. "So awful."

"That's what the police believed," Kelly said, "but they collected DNA from under Rose's fingernails. We think she was pushed and the DNA was from the struggle."

Emma took up the story. "We've been tracking down everyone who was in her class and asking them if they saw anything the night she died. The last night of class."

"Wow. That was a long time ago," Dakota said. "Let me think about it." They all sipped coffee waiting for Dakota to recall anything she could from that night fifteen years ago.

"You know what," she finally said. "I left a few minutes early that night. I had to hurry home to pack for my best friend's memorial service."

"You lost your best friend?" Kelly said sympathetically.

"Yes. In a car accident." Her gaze became curious. "How are you finding everyone? How do you even know who was in the class? Do they keep rosters that long and make them public?"

"We have the class quilt," Emma said. "Everyone signed their block so we have their names. Then it takes good old-fashioned detective work to track everyone down."

"I did an owl block, I remember. In Andy's memory." A pause. "You're not here on vacation. You came to find me."

Emma and Kelly exchanged glances. "Yeah, we did," Emma admitted.

"Yes, and they wore—" Dottie Faye squawked when Emma stepped on her foot to prevent her from telling Dakota about the disguises.

"We're just hoping you can help us," Kelly said hastily.

"I'll give you a DNA sample if that is what you want," Dakota said.

"We can use your napkin," Dottie Faye said, catching on to Emma's pretense that they hadn't tested Dakota. She put out her hand and Dakota gave her the item in question. After locating an evidence collection bag in her roomy purse, Dottie Faye tucked the paper square in and labeled and dated it.

"You're prepared," Dakota said, her eyes widening in amazement. "I didn't know you could use a napkin. I thought it had be a swab or a serious amount of body fluids."

"We like to avoid those," Emma said. "The fluids I mean. You can use a glass or chewing gum or silverware." She deliberately didn't mention the cigarette butt.

"Everything you always wanted to know about DNA collection but were afraid to ask," Kelly cracked. "That's us."

The fake sample safely stowed in Dottie Faye's purse, Emma turned back to the subject at hand. "Did you notice anyone in class who had an argument with Rose? Or anyone who seemed to hold a grudge?"

Again Dakota considered, picking up her spoon and idly stirring her coffee. "Well, there was one girl. Hannah something."

"Hannah Beiler?" Kelly asked.

Dakota snapped her fingers. "That's it. Hannah Beiler. As I recall, she got a D on her final project." She shook her head. "Hannah was not happy about that. Can't say I blame her."

"How did she react?" Emma asked. A bad grade was a thin reason to kill someone, but she'd heard worse.

"She was pretty angry. We sat next to each other, and she spent the last couple of classes glaring at Rose and muttering under her breath."

"Thanks, Dakota. We'll talk to Hannah next."

"How many people have you talked to?"

"You're the seventh. Five more to go, right, Kelly?"

"We've been all over the country and to Europe in pursuit of the truth," Dottie Faye said.

"Dottie Faye's been helping," Emma said, "both financially and otherwise." *And hindering and getting us into trouble and so on,* she silently added.

Dottie Faye nodded graciously. As though in demonstration of her generosity, she grabbed the bill folder from the server and charged the meal to the suite, adding a generous tip.

"I'm impressed by your commitment," Dakota said. "You must have really loved Rose."

"Rose, Kelly, and I were best friends ever since childhood," Emma said. "And obviously we all shared a love of fabric and quilting and sewing. She taught and studied textile design, and we started our quilting store."

Dakota's face darkened. "I've lost people I love too. And also in an untimely and violent manner."

"Like John?" Emma whispered.

Kelly and Dottie Faye looked at Emma curiously but she refrained from explaining, leaving it to Dakota to share whatever she felt comfortable discussing.

Dakota crossed her arms as though hugging herself. It was obviously very difficult for her to talk about him, but once she started, the words came out in a flood. "Yes, John. Like I told you earlier, he was my big cousin and one of my best childhood friends. We grew up together on the reservation just north of Flagstaff. It wasn't the easiest upbringing, especially when I was a teenager interested in boys and partying, but he encouraged me to keep my grades up and go to college. He convinced me that I could be a success, that my weaving had merit. And he helped me get my work into the gallery, since he was part owner. He was with me every step of the way." She shook her head. "I still can't believe he's gone."

"What happened to him?" Kelly asked gently.

"He was shot at his house supposedly during a robbery last week," Dakota said. "The police say he walked in on a burglar. I don't believe it." Anguished tears filled her eyes. "I need to find out who killed him!"

Emma heard an echo of her own fierce determination in Dakota's voice. She put her hand on the other woman's arm. "I understand exactly how you feel. The police won't listen to me, either."

Dakota picked up a napkin and wiped her eyes. "I can't believe I have any tears left."

"Maybe we can help you find out what happened," Kelly offered.

"Really? You would?"

"Absolutely. We have a hundred-percent close rate," Dottie Faye said. "I guess we're just naturally clever, being a lioness, wolf, and fox."

"Oh, your spirit animals." Dakota studied each face in turn. "I can see that."

Dottie Faye swelled with pleasure and patted her mane.

"Tell us more about John," Emma urged. "Who would want to kill him?"

Dakota made a rueful face. "John was fantastic, but he

wasn't the most popular person, if you know what I mean. He spoke his mind and did what he felt was right, despite what others thought. A lot of Navajos regarded him as a sellout because he dealt in art and antiquities. That's a real hot-button topic for us."

"Because of the black market?" Emma guessed. She gave Dottie Faye a meaningful glance, which her aunt ignored.

"Exactly. You aren't allowed to dig up graves or ancient dwellings anymore, especially on government or tribal property. Any artifacts need to have documentation about where they were found and the chain of ownership. John was careful to only sell legal items. In fact, he was an advocate for enforcing the laws. He helped return a lot of gravesite items to the tribe."

"They resented him anyway?" Kelly asked.

"Yes. He was very successful, and that made a lot of people jealous."

"Could that be why his house was robbed?" Emma asked. "He had things someone thought ought to be returned?" She felt a pang of relief. Maybe Dottie Faye didn't have John's stolen bowl, just something similar.

Dakota's next words destroyed that speculation. "I've seen the list of what was taken. There wasn't anything specifically controversial. A couple of valuable items, yes."

"He was a partner in the gallery, right? Does Marc have any ideas?" Recalling the overheard conversation between Dakota and Marc the night of the show, Emma wanted to know more about John's business associate.

Dakota scowled. She seemed to dislike her cousin's business partner. "John just recently became a partner. Back in January, I think. He was really excited at first because it gave him more opportunity to support Navajo artists through shows and introductions to wealthy patrons. But a week or so before he was murdered, he implied he was unhappy about how Marc was running the gallery and his other business affairs. When I pressed him to tell me more, he refused to discuss it. He said he was worried about involving me."

Emma and Kelly exchanged glances. Marc Jacoby sounded like a solid lead. "Unless you know of anyone else who recently threatened John," Emma said, "let's look into Marc."

"I agree," Dakota said. "In fact, there is a two-day tour scheduled to the Double M Ranch, which Marc co-owns. I have to go out there as a guide, and I've heard Marc will be there. Do you want to come along? It'll be fun."

"Will there be cowboys?" Dottie Faye asked with a smirk. "Big, strong cowboys?"

"Absolutely. Real ones. The ranch has roping demonstrations, riding, target shooting, a chuck wagon dinner, and line dancing."

"Target shooting?" Dottie Faye cocked, shot, and blew on an imaginary pistol. "I could brush up on my skills." She cast a critical eye over Emma. "And maybe you can line dance with some of those handsome cowboys. Shake a leg."

"No, thanks," Emma said. "I thought we were going to focus on investigating Marc Jacoby."

"Maybe he dances," the irrepressible Dottie Faye said. "Does he, Dakota?"

"I don't think so." Dakota shot Emma a little smile of sympathy at Dottie Faye's relentless matchmaking and tactfully changed the subject. "As part of the tour, you also get to spend a night in Quincy, a real Arizona mining ghost town. Marc is helping develop Quincy into a tourist attraction, almost like a mini Tombstone."

Emma stopped short before mentioning she'd heard about

the tour at Dakota's presentation the first night—when she supposedly had yet to arrive.

"Marc seems to have his fingers in a lot of pies," Kelly said. "As they say, follow the money. Maybe John uncovered something going on under the table."

"That could be it. Do you know where Marc gets his capital?" Emma asked. "The ghost town attraction alone could cost millions." Tombstone, home of the famous shootout at the O.K. Corral, was a major tourist destination.

"I have no idea," Dakota said. "He hasn't been around more than a few years. I didn't really get to know him until John bought into the gallery. But John did allude to being concerned about Marc's involvement with the ranch and the Quincy project."

"Then it's decided," Dottie Faye said with a slap of her hand on her table. "We'll go on the tour. Where do we sign up?"

Dakota made a quick call to check that there were seats still available on the tour, then left for the gallery with a promise to snoop around in Marc's office if she had an opportunity. Emma, Kelly, and Dottie Faye returned to the suite to freshen up.

"After we sign up for the tour, we can go do our shopping," Dottie Faye said, bustling toward her bedroom. "We'll get you both Western outfits to wear at the ranch."

Collapsing onto the sofa, Emma groaned. "I can't believe I agreed to go shopping. I'd just as soon relax today. I didn't get a wink of sleep last night."

Kelly perched on the other end and idly picked up her phone to check messages. "You know Dottie Faye. Never a dull moment."

As though underlining her words, a shriek rent the air. Emma and Kelly dashed into Dottie Faye's room.

"What's wrong?" Emma cried. "Are you all right?"

Her aunt, still standing upright, appeared unharmed. With a shaking hand, she pointed to the balcony door. As they watched, a strong breeze pushed it open further with a creak. "Someone broke in," Dottie Faye said. "I know I locked that door."

ten

A chill ran down Emma's spine. "Someone tried to get into my room last night too," she said. "Around three a.m."

"Really? Why didn't you say something?" Kelly's expression was appalled.

"I meant to. But I guess I forgot after we got wrapped up in talking to Dakota." Emma glanced around. "Is anything missing, Dottie Faye?" The room looked undisturbed—dresser drawers closed, the bed made, clothes hanging neatly in the closet. Then she realized. A certain cardboard box, which had been sitting on the desk, was gone. "They stole the bowl! The box is gone." Emma felt a wave of relief so intense her knees almost buckled. Now the bowl was someone else's problem.

Dottie Faye laughed. "No, sweet pea. That precious bowl is down in the hotel safe. I took it down to the manager's office late last night, and he put it away while I watched."

Emma and Kelly exchanged confused looks. "You threw away the box, then?" Emma asked.

Dottie Faye shook her head. "No, ma'am. You know that redheaded wig I just got? It itched like the dickens, so I was going to send it back for a refund. That box was just the right size."

"All those wigs itch," Kelly said.

Emma felt lightheaded with incredulous amazement. "You mean the thief stole a wig?"

Dottie Faye cackled in glee. "That's what I'm saying. I sure outwitted that varmint, didn't I?" Her chuckles became an infectious belly laugh, and Emma and Kelly reluctantly joined in. "Can you just picture that little rascal's face when he finally got that box open?" Dottie Faye said, after her laughter wound down. "I used extra strong packing tape, the kind with strings in it. Lots of it too."

The image was amusing. Less so was the realization that Dottie Faye was probably in possession of a murdered man's stolen property. "Dottie Faye, you better sit down," Emma said grimly. There was no easy way to break it to her.

With a flutter of hands, her aunt settled on the bed. "What is it, sweet pea? You don't sound like yourself at all."

Kelly joined Dottie Faye. "You sure don't. What's going on?"

"I'm sure that bowl belonged to John Longbone. The news showed a picture of one just like it that was stolen the night John was killed."

"Why, that can't be," Dottie exclaimed, her face going white behind bright spots of rouge.

Kelly also looked ready to faint. "Maybe it's just a coincidence. There are lots of those bowls around, right?"

Emma paced back and forth across the carpet. "I don't believe in coincidences. The way Percival approached you to buy the bowl, the lack of documentation, the refusal to let you return it—it doesn't paint a pretty picture. It would be bad enough if the thieves were stealing artifacts to sell on the black market, but they apparently graduated to murder."

"Oh, my. What am I going to do?" Dottie Faye wrung her hands as her usual bravado deserted her.

Kelly put her arm around the older woman's shoulders. "We'll figure it out, Dottie Faye. No one will think that you're directly involved in the theft or murder."

"That's true," Emma said. "You were just an overeager collector. I'm sure it happens all the time."

"Should I go to the police? Throw myself on their mercy?"

Emma paced the room again, from bed to dresser to window and back, considering the implications of going to the police. "Not yet," she finally said. "I don't think we should tip the crooks off that way. They have no idea we're helping Dakota investigate John's murder. If we turn in the bowl, it'll be in the papers and everyone will know who we are." She stopped dead, struck by a brilliant strategy. "Besides, if they think we're rich, stupid suckers, we might be able to lure them into a trap."

"Thanks," Dottie Faye muttered.

"In fact, I think we should find Percival and tell him we want to buy more pottery." She dashed over to the phone. "First, let's get the manager up here to report the break-in."

Don Estevez, the day manager, came up to the suite immediately. A tall man with combed-back dark hair and a moustache, he resembled a suave Spanish flamenco dancer with his slender build and quick, lithe movements. "My dear ladies," he said with a slight bow, "I am most distressed that your privacy was breached in this way." He hurried to the door and examined it. "I will have someone up here to reprogram the locks immediately. In fact, we'll replace everything in the suite with upgraded hardware. You were next on the list anyway."

Dottie Faye peered at the electronic mechanism. "I wonder how they did it. Picks are useless on that kind of lock."

The manager cast a curious glance at Dottie Faye, no doubt wondering what such a presumably refined woman knew about picking locks.

"Fortunately, not much was stolen," Kelly put in, to distract the man.

"What exactly is missing? We will provide a list to the

police." Pulling a notepad out of his pocket, he clicked a ballpoint, poised to take notes.

"A wig," Dottie Faye said.

Now Estevez's face was downright puzzled. "A wig? You mean—?"

Dottie Faye swirled her hand around her hair, demonstrating. "Yes, a wig you wear on your head. It was a pretty red-haired one, but it itched something fierce."

"Was it short- or long-haired?"

She frowned, thinking. "Neither. It was kind of medium length. Like a pageboy flip." Again she demonstrated.

Dutifully he wrote the information down, but Emma could tell he didn't exactly hold high hopes for the wig's recovery. He snapped the pen closed and tucked it and the notebook back into his pocket. "I will report the incident to the police."

Dottie Faye put one hand to her chest in a display of feminine gratitude. "I just cannot thank you enough, Mr. Estevez." The accent was back in force, and in addition, her eyelashes batted so hard Emma thought she could feel a breeze. "I was just wonderin' ...."

"Yes, Mrs. Sinclair?"

"I need to speak to that concierge named Percival. You know, the gentleman with the delightful English accent. He promised to get me some particular information about the local area. Do you happen to know if he's working today?"

A strange look crossed Estevez's face. "I'm afraid not, madam. Percival ... ah, left our employ a couple of days ago."

Emma felt a jolt at his words. He must have quit the same afternoon he sent Dottie Faye to buy the bowl. *More evidence that something was wrong. Why else would he suddenly leave such a good job?*

"Shoot! That is a disappointment." Dottie Faye pouted fetchingly.

"Perhaps someone else can help you. What is it you needed?"

Dottie Faye gave a dismissive wave. "Don't bother yourself, Mr. Estevez. I'm sure you're a very busy man. I'll speak to whoever's on duty."

"I'm sure they'll be more than glad to help you." He turned one last time as he reached the door. "Is there anything else I can do for you ladies? If not, please know that there will be a significant discount on your bill."

"Why, that is so kind!" Dottie Faye exclaimed. "Let me walk you out."

She escorted Estevez toward the living room. Emma and Kelly followed.

"We should call Alex," Kelly said, heading for the kitchenette. "You want some cookies? I'm starving." She found a box of homemade treats provided by the resort and opened the lid.

"No thanks. I'm still full from breakfast." Emma perched on a stool at the counter. "What do you want to call Alex about?" Alex Manning, a private detective formerly with the New York City Police Department, had been helping them with the investigation into Rose's death. His contacts gave him access to databases and sources Emma and Kelly couldn't tap.

Kelly set down the white chocolate macadamia nut cookie she'd chosen and ticked off the issues on her fingers. "One, find Hannah Beiler. Two, check out Marc Jacoby. Maybe he can help us find out where Marc came from and where he gets his money." She picked up the cookie and took a bite.

"Good idea. Oh, let's have Alex check out Buck Rodgers too."

Dottie Faye entered the room in time to hear this last bit. "Buck Rodgers? Why on earth would you have a detective investigate him?"

Emma realized she hadn't told the others about the adventures of her early morning run, and she quickly filled them in. "He seems to be following us," she concluded. "He was on the airplane, at the gallery, and is staying here at the resort."

"That's a little far-fetched, don't you think?" Dottie Faye asked. "There are dozens of people you could say the same about."

"I suppose. But even if you're right, it won't hurt for Alex to do a quick identity search on him. And maybe it will put my mind at ease." Emma yawned. "I'm so tired but frazzled at the same time."

Kelly poured herself a tall glass of milk, and then held the container up to see if anyone else wanted some. "No? OK, then." She stowed the milk in the refrigerator. "I suggest we all rest a bit before we go shopping since Emma didn't get any sleep last night. I'll call Alex, and then I'll check in at the store and at home. What do you think?"

"Sounds good to me." Muffling another yawn, Emma slid off the stool. She couldn't wait to lie down and snooze.

"That'll work just fine," Dottie Faye said. She examined her hands critically. "I'll have time to go down and get myself a fresh manicure and pedicure. Then I'll order us a nice room service lunch. We need to keep up our strength for shopping."

Emma groaned. "Oh, yes. Dottie Faye always shops until I drop."

Around one o'clock, the trio sat down to a lunch of white chicken chili, salad, and iced tea on the deck outside the suite.

"Everything here is just scrumptious," Kelly said, pouring blue cheese dressing on her fresh, crisp, colorful salad. "Black olives, avocado, and hot peppers on the salad make it so good."

Emma savored a spoonful of rich, spicy soup. "This soup is just fantastic." She felt much better after her nap, restored to good humor and a fresh appreciation of the beautiful day. The sun shone in a cloudless sky, bringing out the colors of the cliffs and the bright foliage and flowers surrounding the resort buildings. Below the deck, laughing families played in and around the enormous, crystal-blue pool.

"The other services are great too," Dottie Faye said, admiring her fuchsia nails. "My sweet little manicurist told me where to go for the best bargains on Western wear. We'll head over after lunch."

"What did Alex have to say?" Emma asked Kelly.

"He's going to run background checks for all three starting today. He did say it would help to get a little more information about Rodgers, like his given name. He doesn't think he was christened Buck. With Hannah, we know she lived in Mystic Harbor, and Marc obviously lives here in Arizona. We have zero info on Buck."

"I'll try to learn his real name if we see him again," Emma said. "Considering his track record of chasing us around, I'm sure we will."

"I asked Alex about our break-in too. He said some of those locks have a security flaw. Hence the new hardware they put in this morning. Or it could have been an inside job. Someone with a pass key."

Emma shuddered. "Let's make sure we use the deadbolts when we're inside. We don't have anything especially valuable, but I hate the idea of someone trying to come in while we're sleeping. Again."

"Whoever it was must have been pretty darn determined," Dottie Faye said. "We're on the second floor so they had to climb up."

Screams erupted around the pool. The women dropped their silverware, pushed back their chairs, and leapt to their feet to see what was happening.

"I hope no one is hurt," Kelly cried, "or drowning." As a mother, she often feared the worst for her own and other people's children.

Emma pointed to a boy in red trunks brandishing a long silver metal pool cleaning net. "What's he got on the end of that?"

The boy swung and feinted with the pole and its dripping, tangled burden toward other children, who ducked and screamed. A woman on one of the loungers, most likely his mother, threw aside her magazine and came trotting along the concrete pool apron.

Kelly burst out laughing. "I think we've found your wig, Dottie Faye."

After Kelly and Emma rescued the wig and Dottie Faye set it out to dry in hopes it could be restored to a semblance of its former glory, the trio went down to the hotel lobby. Dottie Faye asked the valet for the car while Emma and Kelly approached one of the desk clerks, a young woman with a swishy blond ponytail.

"Excuse me, do you have the itinerary for the Double M Ranch trip?" Kelly asked. "We'd like to sign up." As they drew closer, she noticed the clerk's name tag, which read "Jolie, Salem, Massachusetts." "Hi, Jolie. You're from our neck of the woods."

Jolie's smile was wide in a friendly, open face. "Really? It's always fun to see someone from home." She slid a piece of paper across the countertop. "Here's the itinerary. The tour leaves tomorrow at 8 a.m. And you're in luck—there are still spots open."

"We're from Mystic Harbor," Emma said. "We own a quilt design store there."

"Mystic Harbor? Wow. I love that town. I'll be going home at some point. Probably later this summer when it's slow here. What's your store's name?"

"Cotton & Grace," Kelly said absently, looking at the tour sheet. "This sounds perfect. Look, Emma, the tour includes going to Quincy for a night."

"Quincy is way cool." Jolie's enthusiasm appeared to apply to everything equally. "They have the neatest old hotel there." Her voice dropped to a near whisper. "It's supposedly haunted."

"Great. Another haunted inn," Emma said dryly, referring to Dudley Manor in England where they had stayed while investigating one of Rose's students. "It seems to be a requirement for an inn to have at least one ghost nowadays."

"Yeah, if they don't have any resident ghosts on the property, maybe they advertise the open position," Kelly quipped. "'Ghost wanted.'"

Jolie giggled. "I haven't been to the Hotel Quincy yet, but I plan to stay there next time I go rock climbing with my boyfriend out that way. That's why I moved here—lots of rocks to climb."

"I prefer to look at the rocks from the ground," Kelly said. "Although they sure are gorgeous."

Dottie Faye bustled up to join them, and with her approval of the tour itinerary, all three were soon signed up. "The car's out front," she said. "But before we go, I'd like to ask Jolie something."

"What can I do for you, ma'am? I'm extra-happy to help someone from my hometown," she said. "Well, nearby anyway."

Dottie Faye put on her most sincere, non-conniving expression. "One of your employees was a great help to me the other day, and I'd like to give him a tip."

"That's really sweet. What's his name?"

"I don't know his last name. Percival something. From England." Dottie Faye pointed. "He worked at the concierge station."

For the first time, Jolie's smile faded. "I'm sorry, ma'am, but Percival is no longer with us."

"That's too bad," Dottie Faye said. "Is there any way I can contact him? Telephone? Address? Email even? Though I'd rather see him in person, of course."

Jolie's eyes dropped to the desk. "I'm sorry, we're really not supposed to give out that information."

Somehow a fifty-dollar bill appeared in Dottie Faye's fingers. "That is such a shame," she said. "I believe in tipping generously, especially when staff do me special favors. And he certainly excelled in that department."

Way to lay it on, Dottie Faye! He did you a special favor all right. Emma had to bite her lip to keep from smiling and ruining Dottie Faye's spiel. She noticed Kelly's attempt to hide her amusement by studying their copy of the tour schedule like it held the secret of the universe.

Jolie's eyes were fixed on the money as she wrestled with the temptation to break protocol just once. Finally, seeming to come to a decision, she nodded. Glancing around to be sure no one, especially the manager, was watching, she checked her computer and scribbled on a piece of hotel stationery. "Here's the information you wanted, ma'am." She slid the paper across the countertop to Dottie Faye. "I hope you enjoy the rest of your stay."

In return, Dottie Fay slipped her the fifty. "Thank you,

Jolie. If I happen to see your manager again, I'll tell him what great staff he hires."

"Thank you, ma'am," Jolie said, turning to a man approaching the desk. "How can I help you, sir?"

Emma glanced back. Buck Rodgers again. *Has that man planted a tracking device on us, or is it just a coincidence he turns up everywhere we go?*

She wished she could believe in coincidences.

Emma stared in the mirror, unable to believe her transformation from classic casual woman to cowgirl. She wore a cream-colored embroidered yoke shirt, jeans, and a pale brown cowboy hat with matching boots embossed with a floral design. She put her hands on her hips and stood in a sassy stance, picturing herself as Annie Oakley.

Dottie Faye thrust her head inside the curtain. "Perfect. All you need is a pair of six-shooters hanging off your belt."

Emma shook her head, letting the fantasy dissolve. "No thanks, Dottie Faye. No guns for me."

Dottie Faye withdrew, and Kelly barged into the changing room. She wore a blue embroidered shirt trimmed with mother-of-pearl, jeans, a dark brown hat, and boots. "I can't wait to send the kids a picture. This is fun." She sidled up close to Emma and aimed the smartphone at them. "Smile."

Emma complied. "I never imagined in a million years I'd be wearing a cowboy hat and boots," she admitted. "But it is neat." She flexed her toes in the boots. "And these are surprisingly comfortable."

Dottie Faye joined them, carrying two fringed suede

jackets. Kelly gasped as she handed her the fawn-colored one. "Oh, my. This is just beautiful." Holstering her phone, she slid her arms into the sleeves and posed, turning this way and that. She stroked the soft suede reverently.

Emma put on the dark brown one. "You're right." She threw Dottie Faye a concerned look. "Are you sure you want to do this? The bill is going to be huge."

Dottie Faye clapped her hands in obvious glee at how wonderful her girls looked. "What's the use of money if you don't spend it on those you love?"

Emma gave Dottie Faye a hug. "You are the most generous person I've ever met."

"Pshaw," Dottie Faye said, her face reddening in pleasure. "If your own mama were here, she'd do the same thing."

Emma knew her mother might have wanted to, but the Cotton family budget was much more modest than Dottie Faye's fortune. "Anyway, you certainly have a way of making these trips special and fun."

"That's the secret of life," Dottie Faye said. "Have a little fun on your way down the pike."

"That's a good philosophy," Emma admitted. *I need to remember not to be so focused on the goal that I don't enjoy the journey.* Sure, Dottie Faye had her faults, but she had the rare ability to grab life with both hands and shake out every ounce of pleasure.

Dottie Faye insisted on adding a pair of prairie skirts with flounces and matching embellished tanks to the pile—to wear line dancing, she claimed—before she let them leave the store. She also bought herself a completely black ensemble, including hat and boots. Dottie Faye never wore black. She added silver jewelry as a bright accent, but the effect was still dramatic. "I'm putting the bad guys on notice," she explained as they got into the convertible, loaded down with bags. "There's a new sheriff in town. Miz Dottie Faye Sinclair."

"You tell 'em, Dottie Faye," Kelly said.

"Where to now?" Emma asked.

"I want to find that Percival and get some answers," Dottie Faye said. She handed Kelly the paper Jolie had given her. "Put this address in your GPS, and let's go pay him a call."

Kelly looked at the time on her phone. "It's almost dinnertime. Should we go right now? I'm kind of hungry."

"Yeah, shopping works up an appetite for sure," Emma added. "That soup was quite a while ago."

"Mealtime is the best time to catch someone," Dottie Faye said. "Pick out a restaurant; we'll get takeout on the way back from Percival's house."

Since their route took them along the main route through Sedona, Kelly had great fun calling out the various choices. "Mexican? No, we already had that. Sushi? Nah, not in the mood. Hamburgers? Oh, we'll probably get tons of beef at the ranch." Suddenly she bounced in her seat as they passed a pagoda-style building. "I know. I know. Let's get Chinese!" She turned around in the seat. "Is that OK with you, Emma?"

Emma shrugged. "Sure." She didn't like the fried dishes, but hot and sour soup was a favorite.

"I'd like to get Chinese," Dottie Faye said. "Pot stickers. Crab rangoon. Spring rolls. Teriyaki chicken sticks. Pork fried rice. Uh-huh. That's what I'm talking about."

Kelly rubbed her stomach. "Please. You're torturing me." She glanced at her phone. "Take the next left."

Dottie Faye obediently turned onto the street, which wound away from the main road. Soon they left a neighborhood of single-family homes behind and headed out into the desert. Tumbleweeds rolled along the ditches and in front of the car. The paved road turned into corrugated dirt.

"Are you sure the directions are right?" Emma asked.

Kelly checked the handwritten note again. "Yep. 2111 Ridgeview Court."

"I guess Percy likes his privacy," Dottie Faye ventured. "Living so far out of town."

Finally, several long miles out, they came to a sign that read Ridgeview Court.

"Oh, it's a trailer park," Kelly said.

Dottie Faye slowed the car and turned in, keeping the speed down to 10 miles per hour as they inched along the narrow street. The trailers were generally well kept, some with sunporch and deck additions and lots of lawn decorations and cactus gardens.

"This is probably all I could afford around here," Emma said. Sedona was known for sky-high real estate values.

"They must be boiling hot in the summer," Kelly said, "even with air conditioning."

At the end of a cul-de-sac, they found number 2111, a tiny green trailer with no ornamentation besides a Union Jack on a flagpole attached to the front, like a figurehead on a ship's prow.

"I'm guessing this is it," Dottie Faye said dryly as she pulled to a stop.

"It looks like he's not home," Emma noted. The short driveway and carport were both empty of vehicles, and all the windows were dark. The place had an inexplicable air of desertion.

Emma and Kelly both went to the front door, squeezing together onto a tiny porch. No one answered the doorbell or responded to their knocks on the metal door or the window glass. "I can't see anything," Emma said, peering through the glass. "It's totally dark in there."

"All the rest of the curtains are drawn," Kelly observed. "He's either a really good sleeper or not home."

"Can I help you?" croaked a voice from nearby. They looked over to see an elderly gentleman creeping across the patchy grass between the adjoining trailer and Percival's driveway.

"We're looking for Percival," Emma said, trying to sound like she and the Brit were the best of friends. "Do you know if he's home?"

The man shook his head, not raising his eyes from the shuffling progress of his slipper-clad feet. "He left yesterday." *Shuffle, shuffle.* "Is there anything I can help you with?"

"We hate to bother you, Mr. ...?" Kelly said.

"Just call me Jerry." He had finally reached the porch and now stared up at them with curious eyes behind thick spectacles. Emma had the feeling not much happened out here. They were probably the highlight of his day.

"We're just here to give him a gratuity for helping us out at the resort," Emma said. Perhaps mentioning money would give Percival an incentive to get in touch. "Tell him Mrs. Sinclair was looking for him." She gestured toward the convertible.

"Mrs. Sinclair," Jerry repeated, his eyes following her gesture.

Dottie Faye waved from the convertible, and Jerry's brows rose a bit as he took in her glamorous splendor.

"He can call us at the resort." Emma gave the suite number.

Jerry shook his head. "I'm sorry, miss, but I don't expect to see him again. Last I saw of him, he had his little car piled to the roof with luggage. I think he's gone for good."

eleven

"That was so good," Kelly said, leaning back against the sofa with a sigh. The trio had demolished their Chinese takeout meal; a clutter of white boxes and sauce packets were still spread across the coffee table.

Emma swirled her spoon around the plastic container, spooning up the very last drop of soup. "I'll say. This was made just the way I like it, with lots of mushrooms and bean sprouts. And tofu."

Kelly made a face at the mention of tofu. "That's a little too healthy for me."

Dottie Faye passed around hand wipes, and they all used them, a contented silence falling.

Emma yawned. "I'm going to get an early night, that's for sure. We leave awfully early tomorrow morning."

"What shall we do until bedtime?" Kelly asked.

"There's a good movie on TV in an hour," Dottie Faye said. "Why don't we get comfy and watch it? I have just enough time to run a bubble bath with the relaxing lavender salts I bought at the spa."

"Sounds good," Kelly said, rising to her feet with a groan. She and Emma picked up the trash and tossed it into the brown paper bag the restaurant had provided. Dottie Faye went off to her bathroom, and they heard the thunder of running water.

Emma's phone rang, and an unfamiliar number flashed on the display.

One of the worst effects of their investigation was the trepidation caused by the most ordinary events, thanks to the nasty phone calls and threatening notes they'd received. Answering the phone was especially imbued with a sense of foreboding. Emma stared at the buzzing phone as if it were another rattlesnake in her path.

"Are you going to get that?" Kelly asked as the phone continued to ring.

"I guess so," Emma said, putting it on speaker. This way she wouldn't be alone while enduring the assault of a threat. "Hello?"

"Hi, Emma. This is Dakota."

Emma's shoulders sagged in relief. Friend, not foe. "Hi, Dakota. I didn't recognize the number."

"I'm at the gallery. My cellphone just died, but before it did, I got a call from the police. John's house has been released from being a crime scene."

"That's good, right?"

"I hate to ask you this, but would you go with me over there? I'm really dreading it."

Emma looked at Kelly for input. Her brows furrowed, but then she nodded. "Of course. When did you want to go?"

A gulp was clearly audible. "Actually, I was thinking tonight." Her voice sped up as she tried to explain why. "I know it's short notice and getting late, but I'm going to be away for a couple of days on the ranch tour, and I think I should check it out before I leave. Maybe there will be something helpful that the police overlooked." She gave a strangled laugh. "After all, they just think it was a random robbery. They weren't looking for a connection to Marc, the gallery, or the tribe when they searched his house."

Emma sympathized with Dakota's sense of futility when

it came to convincing the police of anything. *At least there's no doubt it was foul play in John's case. Now we just have to prove who pulled the trigger.*

"We'll go with you, Dakota. Just tell us where to meet you."

"I'll come to the resort and pick you up. How's that? John lives—I mean lived—quite far out." Her voice quivered, obviously on the verge of tears. "Since John was an orphan with no siblings, he left everything to me. So it's my house now, I suppose. If I can stand to live there." With a shuddering gasp, she seemed to pull herself together. "I'll be there in fifteen minutes."

Kelly stuffed the trash into the kitchen wastebasket. "I hope we find something helpful at John's."

"Me too," Emma said, wiping a damp cloth across the coffee table. "Kelly, now your phone is ringing. It looks like Maeve." Kelly had set up her phone to display the pictures of friends and family members when they called. Emma hated the one she chose of her, but Kelly refused to change it, saying it was cute. Emma thought she looked like a demented beaver with her goofy grin.

Swooping back into the living room, Kelly grabbed her phone. "Hey, Mom, what's up?" While Emma watched, her expression changed from casual and happy to troubled concern. "Can you repeat that? Hold on, I'm putting you on speaker."

Alarm ran through Emma like electricity, making her fingertips tingle. "What's wrong?" They'd already endured fire, break-ins, and identity theft.

"It was only by the grace of God I discovered it," Maeve was continuing. "It's a good thing I did, because the water pipe broke today."

Emma shrieked. "The water pipe?"

"Yes," Maeve said. "Water just started gushing into the

basement. Fortunately, I went in early because I was meeting Tokala for breakfast, and I stopped there first. They were able to turn it off within half an hour, so the water was only a few inches deep. The shut-off valve in the basement was broken, so they had to shut it off at the street."

"Any sign of a break-in?" Emma asked. "This wasn't an accident, was it?" She had a sinking feeling that their stalker was behind this latest incident.

"No, it wasn't," Maeve said. "We found a smashed basement window. That's how they got in."

"Why didn't you call us sooner?" Kelly asked.

"We were pretty busy, and I didn't want to ruin your day. There was nothing you or Emma could have done anyway. Patrick and the water guys had the cellar pumped out before noon and set up fans and heaters to dry it out. Nothing was damaged too badly, but the furnace will need to be looked at. The service is coming tomorrow."

"You said you discovered something," Emma asked, remembering Maeve had alluded to a silver lining. "What was it?"

Maeve's voice was grim. "Someone canceled the shop insurance. Any water damage would have been out of pocket."

Emma and Kelly stared at each other in dismayed shock. "What do you mean the insurance was canceled?" Emma almost shouted. "I remember writing the check just a week ago. We've always paid on time. Anyway, there's a grace period."

"When I called the agent to report the flood, they said they were going to return the check since the policy had been canceled. Someone forged the document to authorize it. I got it all worked out, since the agency still had the check. They're going to cover the damages."

"Oh, no," Kelly cried, stamping her foot in aggravation. "How can we prevent something like this from happening again?"

"I did a little research. You should put passwords on all your business accounts. And store the list off-site." A note of satisfaction crept into her tone. "That way no one can mess you about again."

"Good job, Mom," Kelly said. "I don't know how to thank you enough." She collapsed into a chair.

"Maeve, we're so grateful you were there," Emma said. "I don't know what we'd do without you. Please be careful."

"Oh, go on," Maeve said, pleased but bashful at their praise.

"We have to do something nice for your mom," Emma said once the call ended. "She sure saved our bacon." She moved to the sofa, plumping and arranging the pillows. Compulsive neatness was one of the ways she dealt with things like this. The way she felt right now, she could neaten the entire resort.

"I agree," Kelly said. "Let's think of something really special. And I hope we get to the bottom of Rose's death soon so this harassment will stop."

"You think it's related?"

"Absolutely. Why else would we have enemies?" She made a mocking face. "The quilting world isn't exactly cutthroat. We're stepping on someone's toes." She glanced at her phone. "Oops. Time to meet Dakota."

"Good. I don't think I could just sit around here after that phone call."

Dottie Faye wanted to stay behind and enjoy her bath and the movie, so Emma and Kelly left her to it and went down to the lobby to meet Dakota who was parked under the entrance canopy in a white Prius.

"Sorry to keep you waiting," Kelly said. "We had a store emergency."

At Dakota's inquiry, they filled her in on the day's events, in unspoken mutual agreement that it would help her keep her mind off the impending arrival at her cousin's house. The first time visiting the home of a departed loved one was difficult under any circumstances and in this case, incredibly so.

John's house was out in Oak Creek Canyon near Slide Rock State Park. Set on top of a rise with a view of the creek and cliffs beyond, the small home was modern, all angles and glass. "John built it himself," Dakota explained. "Simple design but quality materials."

"It's nice," Emma said, noting the secluded location as they climbed out of the car. The nearest neighbor was out of sight back around a curve in the narrow road. No building, street, or headlights could be seen, and the only sound was wind rustling in the trees and the faint burbling of the creek below.

"It's pretty quiet out here," Kelly said.

"John liked it that way." Dakota sorted through her keys under the motion detector light in the entrance alcove. "You should see the view in the daytime. It's spectacular. Ah, here we go." She unlocked the door and pushed it open. "Let me go first. I need to get the alarm." A light flicked on, and they heard a series of beeps. "OK. All set."

They entered a small square entrance hall, a set of stairs rising to the second story straight ahead. The air had the dank, closed-in smell common to all houses that had been empty for a while.

"Did John always use the alarm?" Emma asked.

In the dim light from the ceiling fixture, Dakota's expression was uncertain. "I'm not sure. I know he did when he wasn't home. I don't know if he bothered when he was here. Anyway, the security company said the alarm didn't go off. They log all those events."

"That's right," Emma said. "Ours at the store does too."

"Were there any signs of a break-in?" Kelly asked.

Dakota shook her head. "No. They didn't find any broken windows or signs that the locks were jimmied. But the sliding door in the den was open. I'll show you." She opened a door on the left into a den with a wide-screen TV and wet bar. She pointed to a tall set of sliders that led to the back yard. Emma and Kelly went to the glass doors and checked them over. A wooden stick lay in the rail to block the door's sliding action, a common deterrent to intruders in addition to the lock.

"That stick wasn't in place?" Emma asked.

"The police said it wasn't. Maybe he left the door open to get some fresh air while he watched TV. I've seen him do that."

"So, either the burglar was incredibly lucky to stumble upon an accessible door when the alarm wasn't set, or it was someone John knew," Kelly said.

"My theory is he knew the person and let them in. Most strangers who break in just do a smash-and-grab, take whatever can be sold easily." She pointed at the TV and stereo equipment. "Like that stuff. A layperson wouldn't understand the value of John's artifacts and antiques or be able to sell them."

"What else is downstairs?" Emma asked as they went back into the hallway.

Dakota opened a door to a small room stuffed with furniture, including an unmade bed, stacked chairs, bureau, and nightstand. "This is a spare bedroom he used for storage. It has its own bathroom. The rest of the space down here is the garage."

Dakota led the way up the stairs, and they emerged into a large open space housing the kitchen, living room, and dining nook. The predominant colors were cream and dark brown accented by touches of pale sage green, giving the room a peaceful mood.

"I love the beamed ceilings," Kelly said. "And the hardwood floors."

"Me too," Emma said, admiring the elegant yet unpretentious style John had chosen. She had a feeling it reflected his personality.

The master bedroom and study were to the right of the stairs, adjoining each other and the main living area. Dakota halted in the study doorway, unable to make herself enter the room where her cousin's life had been so violently taken. She waved a feeble hand. "I can't …. Do you mind?"

"Go ahead and sit down," Emma said kindly. "We'll take it from here."

Dakota quickly moved toward the sofa. "Go ahead and look at whatever you want. The desk, the file cabinets. Anything."

Reaching inside the doorway, Emma switched on the overhead light. Both she and Kelly paused in the doorway, peering inside to get the lay of the room first. A Persian-style carpet lay rolled up on the floor next to the wall.

"I'm guessing that's where—" Kelly whispered.

"Me too." Emma's stomach lurched at the realization that John's blood had stained that rug. How did real detectives and police officers do it? She was far too squeamish. Scolding herself for being a wimp, she walked into the room. On the wall, a safe stood open. From here, it looked empty. Slightly lighter squares on the wall showed where paintings had once hung. The only pictures left were of a man she guessed was John with family, friends, and local dignitaries. He had a wide, handsome face and an irresistible smile. Just from his photograph, Emma liked him. What a tragedy his death was for the people in his life.

"Things are missing out of here," Kelly said. She stood beside a tall glass and wood display cabinet. A few pieces of pottery and several arrowheads were still in the case, but open spots revealed where the more valuable items had once stood.

Like the pottery bowl. It was easy to see where the bowl had been displayed on the top shelf, now entirely empty except for an acrylic stand.

"They obviously knew what they were doing," Kelly added. "How about I start in the file cabinet?" She pulled open the top drawer with a clank of the rollers and began to flip through folders.

"Look for any company agreements or contracts," Emma suggested. "I'll check out the desk." She sat down in the rolling leather chair in front of the glossy mahogany desk. A blotter sat in the middle of the surface, but there wasn't a computer or laptop. The thief or the police must have taken it. She'd have to check with Dakota.

She picked up a small square pad sitting next to the landline telephone. John was a doodler. Every inch of the top page was covered with squares and grids and triangles. She pictured him scratching away while listening to a caller. In the corner was one word, written over and over until it was almost indecipherable. "Kelly, look at this. What do you think it says?"

Kelly took the pad and squinted at the writing before handing it back to Emma. "It looks like 'Quincy' to me."

"That's what I thought." It might mean absolutely nothing more than the old mining town that had been under discussion since Marc was developing it. Emma set it aside anyway.

Kelly handed her a file. "Here's the paperwork I found on the gallery." Inside the folder was a legal document detailing the Sedona Originals partnership agreement. John owned 30%

of the gallery, partially to be paid by commissions on work he brought to the gallery. He'd invested a chunk of cash too. Emma couldn't claim to know much about business deals beyond what she and Kelly had agreed upon, but it looked pretty straightforward to her.

"This is the paperwork for his collectibles company." Kelly passed over another folder. "I'm guessing that's where he got the money to invest in the gallery." This file contained the articles of incorporation for Longbone Collectibles, Inc.

"Have you found any notes about Quincy or the Double M Ranch?" Emma asked.

Kelly shook her head. "The rest of the drawers seem to be paid bills and invoices for the collectibles business, brochures from artists, and that kind of thing."

Emma looked through the desk. Nothing but paper clips, pens, and pencils in the top center drawer, along with a couple of blank message pads. The top drawer on the side held more office supplies, and the one below held a checkbook ledger and an adding machine. "This looks like a dead end."

"If I was suspicious of my business partner," Kelly said, "I'd probably hide my notes."

"Really?" Emma quipped. "Have you given that situation some thought?"

Kelly played along. "Oh, yes. I've started my secret dossier on you, and it's hidden in my freezer."

"I hope Patrick doesn't find it while he's looking for the ice cream."

"No worries. It's in a diet meal box." They both smiled, glad for a little levity to lighten this all-too-serious situation. "I'm going to check out that storage room."

"OK. I'll poke around some more in here. Then I'll look in the freezer." Emma winked.

She looked through the drawers a second time. Nothing of interest. Next she picked up the blotter. Sometimes papers got lost underneath the one on her desk. Nothing but a business card. She picked it up more out of curiosity than any hope it would prove to be significant. The name and title jolted her, and she almost dropped the card.

"Wayne Bryant, Special Agent." The embossed color logo read, "Department of Justice, Federal Bureau of Investigation." John had been in touch with an FBI agent. Could that have something to do with his death?

Emma pushed back her chair with a squeak of the wheels. She had to show this to Kelly right away.

Suddenly, Kelly screamed—a wild, bloodcurdling one that made Emma's hair stand on end.

twelve

Emma bolted from the room, forgetting the business card and its startling revelation that the FBI had been in contact with John. In the living room, Dakota was already moving toward the stairs. They flew down, barely touching the treads, and charged into the guest room.

Kelly stood in front of the big picture window, both hands over her face.

"Are you all right?" Emma cried. "What happened?"

She pointed a trembling finger at the window. "I saw a man out there. He had his hands up to the glass and was peering in at me." She sank down on the edge of the bed.

Dakota pulled her cellphone out of her pocket. "I'm calling the police." She walked a short distance off, and they heard her reporting the incident.

"Do you remember what he looked like?" Emma asked.

Kelly shook her head. "It happened so fast. I caught him out of the corner of my eye, and I screamed. He disappeared immediately."

"How tall was he? Oh, I have an idea." Emma went to the window. Yes, the moist impression of hands and breath still remained. She bent over, matching the imprints on the bedroom side. "Since we're at ground level in this room, it looks like he's about my height."

"The police will be coming right out," Dakota said. She went over to the curtain rod and began to pull the drapes. "We don't need anyone watching us."

"Just a minute," Emma said. She dug a lip salve stick out of her pocket and made an *X* on the window. "This is to show them where exactly he was."

"Good thinking," Kelly said. "You're turning into quite the detective."

"You sure are," Dakota answered. "The only good thing about this is there must be something else here to find or someone wouldn't be snooping around."

Kelly got up. "Let's keep looking." She got on her knees and peered under the bed.

"I'll take the master bedroom," Dakota said, her eyes bright with determination. The awareness that clues may be waiting to be found seemed to have dissolved her understandable distress at being back in John's house.

Emma reinforced Dakota's change in attitude. "It helps to actively seek answers," she said. "It's worked for me, anyway."

Kelly's muffled voice piped up in agreement. "Me too." She backed out from under the bed. "Nope. Nothing here." Still squatted down, she opened the nightstand drawer. "Empty." Then she pulled it right out of its slot. Peering underneath, she said, "Aha! What's this?"

Dakota turned around in the doorway and hurried back to where Emma and Kelly crouched on the rug. "Did you find something?"

"How'd you know to look there?" Emma asked.

Kelly peeled loose the rectangular white business envelope taped to the underside of the drawer. "I've seen this hiding place used on detective shows."

The envelope held photographs, mostly of the desert. Several depicted an old stone building with a metal roof. Behind the ruin stood a distinctive rock spire with a flat rock balanced on top. Kelly passed the photos to Dakota. "Do you recognize this place?"

"No, but I bet it's in Quincy. It looks like an old mining company building."

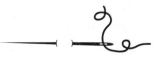

Despite Emma's plans for an early night, by the time they gave statements to the police and finished searching John's house, it was almost midnight. They found nothing new in addition to the photographs and Wayne Bryant's business card.

In the morning, while Kelly and Dottie Faye finished packing, Emma decided to give the FBI agent a call.

"Hello?" His voice was gruff and rusty, like he was still half-asleep.

"Oh, did I call you too early?" Emma chirped. "I thought all FBI agents got up early. To get their man and all."

"Who is this?"

"Emma Cotton."

"Do I know you?" he barked.

His harsh tone set her nerves on edge, and her plan to stay cool evaporated. "Probably not. Definitely not. I'm helping a friend with her cousin's death, and I was wondering if you knew anything about it."

Emma could almost hear his wheels turning as he considered her words.

"Who's the cousin?"

"John Longbone."

If he was stunned before, now he was completely dumbfounded. Amazing how that translated over the telephone.

Maybe it was his stuttering gasps for air that gave his confusion away.

Emma waited. Any second now he would rally and chew her out for meddling in his case. *10, ... 9, ... 8, ...*

"Look, Ms. Cotton, I don't know what you're up to, but you had better not be interfering in an official investigation. Butt out."

"Really? Is there an FBI investigation? I thought they believed he was killed in a random robbery. Is the FBI solving local robberies now?" Emma knew she shouldn't poke at him, but there was just something about his arrogance that made her want to get under his skin.

"I really can't discuss it. For your own safety, I'm warning you to drop it."

"OK," Emma lied, smiling internally. He had admitted that the FBI was interested in John's death. That meant crime on a much higher level.

"Where did you get my number anyway?"

"I found your business card on John's desk," Emma said. She heard another intake of breath as he prepared to ratchet up the dressing-down. "I'm helping his cousin, Dakota, settle the estate," she quickly added. "We came across it while we were cleaning up. I thought you might know something to put poor Dakota's mind at ease. For instance, the imminent arrest of the murderer. I mean, there must have been a reason for John to have your number. Was he in trouble?" She could wiggle and maneuver with the best of them. All part of the sleuthing game, not something that she normally subscribed to, of course.

"I'm sorry, Ms. Cotton," he said after another short silence, "but I can't discuss this with you. Have a nice day."

He hung up, and Emma stared at the phone, ticked off at

his rudeness and at the general reluctance of law enforcement to listen to civilians. Deputy Chief Tom Boyer back in Mystic Harbor wasn't quite as brusque, but he certainly continued to stonewall her urgings to reopen Rose's case.

It must be nice to be so certain that your judgments and decisions are always correct. Keeping an open mind worked better for her. Maybe it was petty, but Emma looked forward to the day when Tom Boyer had to admit she had been right all along about Rose's case. And after this phone call, she felt exactly the same about Wayne Bryant's comeuppance.

"Are you ready to leave?" Kelly asked, emerging from her bedroom. Wearing her cowboy hat and fringed jacket over jeans, she pulled a suitcase behind her, the wheels making tracks in the plush carpet.

Emma slid her phone into her handbag. "Yes. My suitcase is already in the hall on the rolling cart. By the way, I just got off the phone with Wayne Bryant. I think he's investigating John's death. Of course, he didn't come right out and say that. But he sure didn't like me asking questions."

Kelly laughed. "Do they ever? But that's not going to stop us." From the recesses of Kelly's own handbag, a ringtone piped. She dropped the suitcase handle to dig around for her cellphone. "Oh, good. It's Alex. That was quick." She pressed the button to connect. "Good morning, Alex. Emma's here with me, and I have you on speakerphone. Any luck?"

An exasperated sigh came over the speaker. "I suppose you could call it that. Sometimes it's more what you don't find that tells the story."

Emma and Kelly exchanged looks. "What do you mean?" Emma asked.

"I can't find a trace of Marc Jacoby anywhere before his arrival in Sedona three years ago. Nothing in the vital records.

No school, employment, or even a driver's license. I think he must be using an alias." He gave a short laugh. "Or he's in the witness protection program."

"Maybe so," Kelly said. "Once a crook, always a crook, right?"

"That is really suspicious," Emma said. "Nowadays people usually leave some kind of trail."

Alex sighed again. He always took it as a personal affront when the records and databases didn't yield the answers he wanted. "And I didn't have a bit of luck with the Beiler woman either. There aren't that many Beilers outside of Amish country. That's about all I know. I'm batting a thousand here."

"Thanks for trying, Alex. We'll do some more research and try to pick up Hannah's trail when we get back home." Kelly grimaced at Emma. "After Easter. And a break from traveling."

"Dakota Longbone wasn't the one, huh?"

"No. We already got the DNA sample back." Emma remembered her last request to Alex. "I don't suppose you had any luck with Buck Rodgers?"

"Afraid not. You'll need his real first name. Buck has to be a nickname since I couldn't find him anywhere. Let me know if you get it."

Emma hoped they wouldn't see Buck again. Otherwise his constant presence was just too weird to be a coincidence. "Sure, if I can. Hey, guess what? We've got a FBI agent hanging around. His name is Wayne Bryant. Do you think you can find out what angle he's working?"

Alex whistled. "I can try, but the feds don't like to give out case info. Something going on down there has the big dogs involved, huh?" His voice brightened. "Maybe he's investigating Marc. That would make sense."

"Maybe so. Dakota Longbone's cousin was murdered. And he's the one who had Bryant's card."

"Heavy. Well, ladies, call if you need anything else. If you find out anything more about Hannah Beiler, let me know so I can narrow the search. Many of the Amish are off the grid, so it's needle-in-a-haystack time. But I'll keep digging and see if I can find out anything else."

Shortly after hanging up with Alex, Dottie Faye finally finished packing. After maneuvering the laden baggage cart into the elevator and down the hall to the lobby, they piled everything into the rental car. According to Jolie, their new desk clerk friend, the barbershop quartet and their wives had taken the resort van to the ranch. Their party could have done the same, but Dottie Faye assured Jolie that she preferred the freedom and flexibility of having her own car.

"An escape vehicle," Kelly muttered under her breath.

With a final wave and smile for Jolie, they climbed into the car to head out, Dottie Faye at the wheel, resplendent in her white cowboy hat. To join the other two, Emma put her hat on too, smiling at the thought that modern cowgirls rode the type of Mustang that chewed up gas, not hay. Away from the building, Dottie Faye picked up speed as she cruised along the winding resort road. Emma felt a resulting tug on the wide-brimmed hat, and she quickly clamped her hand on the crown to press it more firmly in place. "Maybe we should put the top up," she called to Dottie Faye from the back seat. "Or slow down. I don't want to lose my hat."

Dottie Faye hit the brakes, jerking them forward against the seatbelts.

"I didn't mean slow down that much!" Emma protested.

"Sorry," Dottie Faye said. "I hit the brakes a little too hard." She increased speed slightly. "Do you recognize that man over there? The one operating the leaf blower?"

Off to their right, a thin man wearing a resort uniform

and ear protectors swung a leaf blower across a concrete path outside one of the resort buildings. Sensing their eyes on him, he looked up and scowled.

"I've never seen him before," Kelly declared. "He's pretty average, so I can't say for sure."

He turned his back on them and walked the other way, sending leaves and grass clippings into the flowerbeds bordering the walkway.

"I don't recognize him either," Emma said. "Maybe you've just seen him working around here."

"It's going to bug me until I remember," Dottie Faye said. She stopped at the resort gate and checked traffic before proceeding onto the road to town. "I know I've seen that skinny little behind somewhere." She mused some more, muttering under her breath. Then she snapped her fingers. "That was Fiske—the little weasel who drove me to buy that illegal old bowl."

thirteen

"**M**aybe we should go back and talk to him," Kelly suggested.

Emma considered Kelly's idea, tempted herself to try to get some answers from Fiske regarding the whereabouts of Jim Smith, the owner of the warehouse where Dottie Faye had purchased the bowl. But why tip their hand? She recommended they let the thieves think they were just ignorant, innocent tourists without an inquisitive bone in their bodies. "He was just the driver," she added. "Maybe he doesn't know anything, anyway. If we need to, we can always talk to the manager about him when we get back." *By then, it might be time to come clean about the bowl—if we don't have any luck at the ranch or in Quincy.*

Kelly echoed her thoughts. "I hope we get this whole thing wrapped up by then."

The twenty-mile trip to the ranch led them south into the desert. One by one, jutting rock formations appeared in the distance, growing larger as they drew closer, then receding behind, others taking their places. Meadows of purple and yellow flowers sprawled below towering stands of saguaro cacti. Nothing moved in the quiet landscape, although an occasional turkey vulture or hawk circled above, riding the wind currents.

Emma sat back and savored the experience of observing country so different from green and lush New England. There the hills rolled softly, cradling villages and towns in protective hollows. In contrast, this view and sky were wide open, a magnificent panorama that made it quite clear how puny humans actually were when moving across the vast reaches of the desert.

Cattle grazing on dun-colored hillsides were the first sign they were approaching the ranch. Dottie Faye slowed and turned onto a wide dirt road marked by a wooden arch reading Double M Ranch.

"I'm excited," Kelly said. "I've never been to a ranch before. I feel like I'm in a Western movie."

More cattle grazed on both sides of the road, hemmed in by miles of metal fence. In the distance, a lone cowboy rode among the herd on a four-wheel ATV, not a horse.

"There goes that illusion," Emma said.

"They probably save the horses for the guests," Dottie Faye said. "ATVs are practical on rough terrain."

"You sound like you know what you're talking about," Kelly said.

"Oh, an old friend of mine owns a ranch in Texas. Swears by 'em."

"I thought you were going to say you've worked on a ranch," Emma said. "You've done just about everything else."

"Don't you know it? But no, ranching isn't in my skill set. Yet."

They passed under another arch and entered the sprawling, multi-acre ranch compound. The main area held a two-story ranch house, bunkhouses, outbuildings, and barns, all in natural wood with green metal roofs. Down a path, Emma saw small cabins placed among a grove of cottonwood trees. Corrals lay beyond the biggest barn, and parked beside it was a covered wagon.

Dottie Faye stopped in front of the main house, near steps leading to the wide front porch. Beside the steps, a flag reading Office hung in a bracket from one of the posts.

Inside the front door was a small reception area next to a flight of stairs. In the room to the right was a gift shop; on the left was a long living room dominated by a huge fieldstone fireplace. With wood floors and paneling and accents of red in the cushions, curtains, and rugs, the place had a rustic but homey feel. No one was around, so Dottie Faye rang the push-button bell.

"Look at that quilt," Kelly said. Emma followed her gaze to a quilt displayed on the wall of the living room. It was an eight-pointed star design in alternating red and brown calico. Floral print squares provided contrast.

"It's lovely," Emma said, drawn to the quilt as though by a magnet. While quilts of all vintages were lovely, even stunning, there was something special about antiques. Often faded and slightly yellowed, as this one was, Emma was awed by the connection they provided to the past, to the women who had so diligently pieced and quilted scraps of cloth into works of art.

"It's one of my favorite patterns," Emma said. "Star of Bethlehem. Eastern Star. Lone Star. It has many names."

"It's got to be mid-1800s," Kelly said, "judging by the fabric."

"1848, to be exact," a friendly female voice behind them said. "Bill's great-great-grandmother brought it with her from back East when they settled this land."

They turned to see a middle-aged woman with cropped curly dark hair, dressed in jeans, sweatshirt, and sneakers. She smiled. "I'm Marge Marshall. My husband Bill and I own the place. I take it you're interested in antique quilts?"

"Oh, yes," Emma said. She introduced herself and the others and told Marge about their store.

"Well, maybe I can pull out a couple more for you to look at later on," Marge said. "Let's get you settled first." After they signed in, she took a key off the board behind the desk. "I've put you in The Pokey. It's a nice little place."

"Um? The pokey?" Kelly said. "Isn't that the jail?"

Marge laughed. "Yep. We gave the all cabins Western names, just for fun." She waved the key. "Don't worry, you'll be able to unlock The Pokey from the inside."

Once outside on the porch, Dottie Faye asked where they should park the car. Marge told her someone would park it for her, motioning toward a nearby lot. Glancing that way, Emma saw Marc Jacoby getting out of his white Jeep. Emma still had questions about Marc. Marge was saying they'd get one of the "cowpokes" to take their luggage to the cabin. She whistled a shrill two-fingered chirp and waved at a cowboy approaching on horseback. As he guided the horse to a stop next to the car, Emma realized it was Buck Rodgers, the man they seemed to see everywhere.

What the heck is he doing here? Surely it wasn't a coincidence that he'd approached the desk clerk right after they had made arrangements for the tour. He had to be following them. Fear lanced through her gut. Did he have something to do with Rose's death?

"Buck will take your bags to the cabin," Marge was saying when Emma tuned back in, unable to stop staring as the cowboy deftly swung out of the saddle and tied the reins to the porch rail.

"Howdy, ladies," he said with a tip of his hat. "Good to see you again."

"What are you doing here?" Emma blurted, despite her efforts to keep quiet. She heard the edge to her tone and bit her tongue. If he were stalking them, it would be safer to pretend that she didn't realize it.

A flash of anger raced across his face so fast she wondered

if she had imagined it. "I'm just enjoying visiting this fine ranch," he said, his slight accent thickening into a drawl. "How 'bout you?"

"Buck is here for the 'work on a ranch' package," Marge explained. "We're having him do a little of this, a little of that, right, Buck?"

"That's right, ma'am. It's giving me a taste of real ranch life. I'm getting a hankering to buy one and retire."

Dottie Faye batted her lashes. "I'm awfully glad to see you again, Buck. I've got a sweet spot for cowboys. Even those in training."

"And I'm sure they have a sweet spot for you," he said gallantly. He pulled two suitcases out of the trunk as easily as if they were empty, but he looked startled when he saw the rest of the luggage Dottie Faye had brought along. "I'll just get the wagon and bring all this down to the cabin. Which one is it, Marge?"

"The Pokey. See you in a few." She herded them toward the path, but Emma darted back and grabbed the laptop case before following the others. They'd had people steal computers before, and she wasn't letting this one go.

A short distance away, a crowd was clustered around a corral, hooting and cheering at riders circling around a long-legged calf.

"What are they doing?" Emma asked.

"We're holding a rodeo clinic this week to teach roping skills," Marge explained. "That class is full, but you can take a riding lesson or go for a trail ride. We also have a shooting range if you want to get in a little target practice. If you've never handled a gun, we can teach you to shoot. And if you feel like just kicking back and relaxing, we have real nice rocking chairs on every porch."

"I've handled both horses and guns," Dottie Faye said, puffing her chest with pride. "In fact, I'm known far and wide for my skills."

"Indeed she is," Emma said, at seeing Marge's eyebrows rise in disbelief that a Southern lady like Dottie Faye would clamber up on the back of a horse or handle a gun. "In fact, we have to restrain her from adding to her extensive collection of firearms."

Dottie Faye ignored that. "Tell me, Marge, are any of your good-looking cowboys going to be giving us lessons?"

"Oh, all our instructors are good-looking, especially my husband, Bill."

"It must take a lot of hands to keep this place going," Kelly said.

"It sure does. We have over 40,000 acres." Now Marge was the one speaking with pride. "Although we have guests and lots of fun activities, it's a real working ranch. Our cattle are prized both as breeding stock and for their tender meat. You'll get to taste some of our best steaks tonight at our chuck wagon supper." Marge chuckled. "Then you can burn off the calories line dancing."

"My mouth is watering already," Kelly said. Her stomach growled, and she put a hand over it in embarrassment. "Sorry. Breakfast was a while ago."

"Lunch is in an hour," Marge said. "At the pavilion behind the big barn." She stopped in front of one of the cabins, which indeed did have four rocking chairs placed along the front porch. "Here we are. The Pokey." She unlocked the door and stood back to let them in.

The main room of the small cabin was paneled in wood and furnished country-style with ruffled curtains, pleasantly shabby upholstered furniture, and bright rag rugs here and there on the pine floor. Off this central area were two bedrooms and a bathroom tucked in between. "It's simple—no telephone or television—but it's comfortable," Marge said. "If you need anything, feel free to come by the office."

"Everything looks lovely," Dottie Faye said. "I think I'll try out one of those rockers while we wait for our luggage." She followed Marge back outside.

"It's a lot less plush than the suite at the resort," Kelly said, "but I like it." She peeked inside one of the bedrooms, which held a bunk bed made up with cozy patchwork quilts. The pictures on the wall and the lamp on the bedside table had a vintage cowboy theme. "Dibs on the top bunk."

"Good," Emma said. "I'm afraid of heights, so I'll take the bottom one."

Kelly hooted. "Seriously, Emma, you're afraid of sleeping in the top bunk?"

"Yes, I am. Remember the time we went away to camp? I had the top bunk, and I couldn't sleep all night. I kept feeling like I was going to fall off."

"Oh, yeah. I do remember that. Didn't Rose trade with you?" Kelly went to the window and checked the view of pastures and grazing cattle.

"Yes, she did. She was a *nice* friend." Emma's tone was teasing. She sat on the bottom bunk and bounced, testing the mattress. "Not bad." She gazed around at the decor. "I feel like I'm in a 1950s boy's bedroom." She tugged the braided horse-hair pull that turned the lamp on and off.

"It's cute, isn't it? When Keith was little, cowboys were passé. It was all Ninja Turtles and Power Rangers." Kelly leaned against the window, wistful for a moment. "What was up with you and Buck earlier?" she asked. "I thought you were going to take his head off."

"Don't you think it's strange that he's here at the ranch?" Emma ticked off the places they had seen him, starting with the plane. "It's like that credit card ad—he's everywhere we want to be."

"He hasn't done or said anything threatening, has he?"

"No," Emma had to admit. "He actually helped me once, when I almost stepped on that snake."

"Those barbershop quartet folks are around a lot too. Do you think they're following us?" Despite the chiding words, Kelly's tone was gentle. Usually Kelly suffered from an overactive imagination and Emma reassured her. She finally had the chance to return the favor.

"Of course not." Emma frowned down at the rag rug, pretending to examine the seemingly random but eye-pleasing way the bright colors worked together. She felt foolish for suspecting Buck of criminal intent. Was working on Rose's case causing her to see imaginary threats and evil plots where none existed?

Kelly's next words surprised her. "Maybe he is following you … because he likes you."

Reluctant laughter burst out of Emma. "Oh, come on. That's ridiculous."

"Really? Why? You're beautiful. And he's not bad-looking, either, especially on horseback." Kelly whistled.

"Being around Dottie Faye too much is softening your brain." Sometimes she thought she should get married, just to get Dottie Faye and Kelly off her back. Then they'd have to find a new hobby besides trying to matchmake for her. At the sound of voices in the main room, she cocked her head, listening. "It sounds like Dakota made it."

They went out to the main room, and the first thing Emma did was check over the pile of luggage by the door.

"Everything there?" Kelly teased as she plopped onto the sofa beside Dakota.

Emma flushed but continued to pull apart the pile and sort by owner. Yes, she noted with relief, Buck had brought everything. She covered her actions by pulling her suitcase handle out so she could wheel it along. "We're in the bunk room," she told Dottie Faye and Dakota. "So I guess you two are sharing the other room."

"Sounds fine to me," Dakota said. "The special tour has us here just for tonight anyway."

"I'm looking forward to a riding lesson this afternoon," Emma said after she parked the bag in her room and joined the others. "I haven't been on horseback for ages."

"I'll never forget the last time I went riding. It was with Julie," Kelly said. "My daughter," she added for Dakota's benefit. "When she turned twelve, she went through a horse-crazy phase like a lot of girls and insisted on riding lessons. Once, only once, she dragged me along. The nag they gave me wouldn't lift his head." She mimed tugging on the reins. "Halfway through the ride, he bolted back to the barn through the woods! A low-hanging branch almost wiped me right off his back. I still think that might have been deliberate."

Everyone laughed. "The horses here are a lot nicer," Dakota promised. "I recommend that you all take a lesson today. Horseback is the best way to explore Quincy. It's much less obvious, and some of the old mining roads are impassable by car anyway."

"We'll do that, right after lunch," Kelly said. "Which I hope is any minute now. I'm absolutely famished."

The clanging of a percussion triangle echoed through the ranch.

"There's our cue," Dakota said, rising to her feet. "The dinner bell."

"Gosh, I'm sore," Kelly said as she, Emma, and Dottie Faye plodded back to the cabin. "Riding uses muscles I forgot I had. And ones I never knew I had."

"I agree," Dottie Faye said with a groan. "Did you notice if the bathroom had a tub? I want a long, hot soak before dinner."

"Yes, it does," Emma said. She was the only one walking fully upright and at her usual pace.

Kelly gave Emma a glare. "I suppose you're not sore."

"I am, a little," she said, rubbing her behind in solidarity with the others. In truth, her running and yoga routines kept her limber. "It was fun, though."

They'd started off with a few circles around the corral so the riders and horses could get used to each other. Then the instructor—a woman, to Dottie Faye's chagrin—led them and a dozen other guests, including the barbershop quartet couples, on a short trail ride offering fine views of Sedona's red rocks in the distance. Emma thoroughly enjoyed ambling along on her palomino mare, feeling warm spring sunshine on her shoulders and breathing in mingled scents of sagebrush, leather tack, horseflesh, and fresh air. Her mount's mane gleamed bright white in the sun, a nice contrast to her gold coat that felt like warm satin under Emma's palm.

"It was great," Kelly agreed. "At least this time my horse didn't try to throw me off or anything. And Dottie Faye, you were fantastic."

The older woman lived up to her claim of riding expertise when she led her pretty little buckskin through her paces—walk, trot, canter, and gallop—in front of an admiring audience. Even the instructor had been impressed. "Why, thank you. I guess it's kinda like riding a bicycle. You never forget."

"I think it's a little harder," Emma said. "After all, bicycles don't buck or bite."

The sound of the barbershop quartet singing *The Yellow Rose of Texas* greeted them as they approached the chuck wagon in the covered pavilion behind the big barn.

"Wow. There sure are a lot of people here," Emma said. More than a hundred people of all ages sat at the picnic tables or stood in line at the covered wagon serving station. "They're not all staying here, surely."

"The parking lot looks full," Kelly said. "I think people must come out from town for these suppers." She took a sniff. "And I can't say I blame them. It smells fantastic."

Indeed, the mouth-watering odor of grilling meat hung heavy in the air.

Dottie Faye inhaled deeply. "I smell ribs." Emma and Kelly both gave her a bemused look. "A Southern gal can identify a barbecuing rib with one breath," Dottie Faye explained. "And the style." She took another sample of air, her nose twitching. "They used a wet sauce."

Emma shook her head. "Dottie Faye, you are amazing."

Marge stood where the food line formed, taking tickets and greeting people. Next to her, a pleasantly stout man wearing Western garb and a cowboy hat, like most of the guests, helped out. "Evening, ladies," Marge said. "This is my husband, Bill." She introduced everyone. "Since you're staying here, you don't need tickets."

"We've got steak, ribs, and chicken on the grill," Bill said. "Whatever your heart desires."

Dottie Faye smirked in triumph. "Wet sauce, right?"

Bill nodded. "Yes, ma'am. Our own sweet and tangy family recipe."

Kelly moaned. "Oh, yum. I had my heart set on the steak, but now I don't know."

"Have them all," Marge suggested.

Bill pointed to a huge cauldron supported by a frame and chain. "We've got real bean-hole beans." He winked. "Made with another family recipe. They've been simmering underground for the past sixteen hours. Plus corn on the cob, green salad, and baked taters."

"Don't forget the biscuits," Marge added. "And for dessert, we're serving our famous apple crisp. With fresh cream or homemade ice cream."

"Good thing we worked up an appetite riding today," Dottie Faye said.

Emma felt her belt tightening around her waist just at the thought of all that delicious food. Kelly looked ready to faint with anticipation.

They were able to find empty seats in the far corner for all of them, including Dakota, who planned to join them after finishing her tour-related tasks in the ranch office. Emma selected a modest helping of steak, corn, salad, and beans; Dottie went for the ribs, salad, and a baked potato; and Kelly, of course, took a small helping of everything, resulting in a well-mounded plate. A couple of men observed her carrying the load with both hands and appeared impressed. "I like a woman who's not afraid to eat," one called.

"So does my husband," Kelly said with a laugh.

"Lucky man," the other replied.

"No wonder the men are flirting with you, Kelly," Dottie Faye said after they settled in their seats at the picnic tables. "You're just as cute as a button in that cowgirl getup." She cast a skeptical eye on Emma. "You're cute too, but you've got to get yourself out there."

Emma poured three glasses of ice water from a pitcher set on the table and passed them around. "Believe it or not, I'm happy just the way I am." Picking up her knife and fork, she cut a piece of thick, tender steak, cooked medium rare, just the way she liked it.

Dottie Faye gave a snort at Emma's folly before turning to her meal. "Uh-huh!" she exclaimed after chewing a bite of rib. "That's what I'm talking about."

"I'm in heaven." Kelly slathered butter on the baked potato and corn, then sprinkled salt and pepper liberally over everything. "This is just perfect."

Finished collecting tickets, Marge and Bill were circulating around the tables, chatting and laughing with their guests. As they made their way toward the trio, Kelly wiped her hands on a napkin and reached into the back pocket of her jeans. She pulled out the photo of the old mine building and flashed it at Emma and Dottie Faye.

"What are you doing?" Emma asked.

"I'm going to ask them if they know where this is."

"Are you sure it's a good idea to let people know we're interested in it?" Emma whispered.

"I have a cover story. You'll see." She put on a big smile as the couple approached.

"Enjoying the meal, ladies?" Bill asked. They all made murmurs of appreciation.

"Don't forget to visit the dessert table," Marge said.

"I won't," Kelly said. "Not sure about these wimps." She grinned at her companions. She handed Marge the photo. "Do you know where this is? My son was on a trip out here last year and took this picture. He said it was a really cool place to visit, but he couldn't remember exactly where this building was located."

Marge pursed her lips, frowning. "That's part of the old Quincy silver mine. It hasn't been in operation for decades. But you don't want to go out there."

"Why not?" Kelly asked.

Bill edged onto the bench next to Kelly while his wife perched beside Dottie Faye. His broad, friendly face grew grim as he spoke. "There are a lot of old mine shafts in the area. If you fell in one ..." He shook his head and whistled.

"People have died out there," Marge stated baldly. "Your son is lucky he didn't meet with an accident. People are riding or walking along when suddenly—boom—they fall into a shaft filled with water. Even if they yell for help, no one can hear them hundreds of feet underground. They can't climb out, so they get tired and drown. Even if someone does call 911 for help, it can take hours for a rescue crew to arrive so far out in the desert."

Thanks to her excellent imagination, Emma could picture the horrific scene all too well. Her stomach clenched in fear and revulsion as Marge continued her gruesome warning. "Even worse, some of those old shafts and tunnels collapse, sending a ton of rocks and dirt down on top of folks." She shook her head. "Those bones will never be found." She leaned across the table, fixing Emma and Kelly with fierce eyes. "Stay away from that mine. I don't want to track you folks by watching for turkey buzzards circling overhead."

fourteen

"We don't mean to scare you, but we have to keep our guests safe," Bill said. At Emma's shocked silence, he gave an uneasy chuckle. "I'm sure you understand."

"That's right," Marge said. "We don't want anyone to get hurt." She slapped the table and stood up. "Enjoy the rest of your dinner."

"Not likely," Emma said after the couple sashayed over to another table. She pushed her plate away, unable to eat another bite.

"That was downright strange," Dottie Faye mused. "All it did was strengthen my curiosity about that little ol' mine."

Carrying a plate of food, Dakota wound her way through the tables and slid into the seat beside Dottie Faye. "Sorry I'm late. I'm glad they still had something left with this crowd." In the middle of unrolling her silverware from a napkin, she noticed their glum attitude. "What's wrong?"

Emma shared Marge's warning with Dakota, who shrugged. "Don't worry about it," Dakota said. "I have a geological survey map of Quincy that shows all the hazards." She took a bite of steak and chewed with enjoyment. "Yum. This just melts in your mouth, doesn't it? Listen, I'm more convinced than ever that there is something funky about that mine building." She lowered her voice. "One, why would John hide a picture of it, and two, why would you be warned away so strongly?"

"You're right," Kelly said, picking up her fork. "Marge's story was really over the top. She should write thriller movies."

She attacked her supper with renewed gusto. "Hey, Emma, if you're going up for dessert, can you get me one?"

"I wasn't. But sure, I'll go get you a bowl. Dottie Faye? Dakota?" Emma stood up, gathering the empty plates and cups for disposal.

Dottie Faye shook her head. "No thanks, sweet pea. I'm full."

"I don't think I have time," Dakota said. She glanced at her watch. "I have a Navajo legends presentation in fifteen minutes or so out by the bonfire." She quickly ate the last few bites of her meal. "But I do have just enough time to grab a cigarette. Want to come with me, Dottie Faye?"

Emma's mind raced back to Dottie Faye's ruse of sharing a smoke break to get to talk to Dakota. Biting her lip to stifle nervous laughter, Emma stopped clearing the table to watch how Dottie Faye handled Dakota's request. Kelly, too, was struggling to keep her face straight. Her aunt rose to the occasion with surprising aplomb. "I appreciate that, Dakota, but I quit. Cold turkey."

"Really? When?"

Dottie Faye gave her a good imitation of a sincere smile. "Yesterday."

Dakota studied Dottie Faye's calm demeanor. "You're doing great. Last time I tried to quit, I was a real grouch. Aren't you a nervous wreck?"

"She hides it well," Kelly said, darting a sly glance at Emma. "Underneath, she's just seething, aren't you, Dottie Faye?"

"That's right, Kelly. I'm just a bundle of nerves. But with maturity comes greater self-control. As I'm sure you'll learn someday." Dottie Faye smirked with satisfaction at her dig as Kelly feigned injury with a pout and a hand to her chest.

Not seeming to notice the banter, Dakota rose from the

table, grabbing her own empty plate and water glass. "I'm trying to quit too. Maybe you can give me some tips."

"Oh, my," Dottie Faye said once Dakota was out of earshot. "Where am I going to get tips on quitting smoking?"

"Want me to check Google?" Kelly offered. "I'll search while I'm looking for advice on how to become more mature." The trio burst into laughter.

After Kelly finished her second helping of apple crisp, they hurried over to the bonfire to catch Dakota's presentation. The crowd sat around the fire on long peeled logs and folding chairs. Dressed in knee-high moccasin boots, a pleated red velvet skirt with a sash belt, gold blouse, and heavy turquoise jewelry at her neck, ears, and wrists, her long gleaming hair swinging free, Dakota was a vision of Native American beauty. To Emma's delight, she discovered that her new friend was a talented storyteller. The audience listened in rapt silence as her funny, touching, and frequently sad tales featuring the trickster coyote carried them into the heart of Navajo culture. Overhead, stars sprinkled the inky sky like silver confetti. Emma sensed the vast, empty spaces surrounding their friendly, safe circle clustered around the bonfire's light and heat. For centuries, Emma thought, the people of this land gathered in much the same way, united in their enjoyment of story and fellowship.

After Dakota finished, the crowd broke into applause, some young men at the back adding hoots and hollers. "Wasn't that grand," Bill Marshall said, replacing Dakota as she slipped away with a final wave and smile. "While we get the barn ready for line dancing with the Honky-Tonk Rodeo Show band, on tour from Phoenix, we'll be serenaded by our guests, the Lone Star Warblers, a fabulous barbershop quartet from, you guessed it, Texas." Everyone clapped. Bill held up a hand. "But first, a word from our sponsor." With a smirk, he gestured for someone to move into the firelight.

"I hate it when you introduce me that way, Bill." Marc Jacoby, elegant and urbane in head-to-toe silver-gray Western wear, stepped forward. "Howdy, folks. I'm Marc Jacoby, and despite what Bill says, I'm just a minor partner in all this." He waved his hands expansively. "Isn't this just a fabulous ranch?"

"Yes!" the crowd yelled.

"Bill and Marge do such a good job out here. And wasn't that meal fantastic?" Marc rubbed his stomach in appreciation. "I know I ate too much." Everybody laughed, and a few people clapped.

Despite the doubts about Marc Jacoby created by John Longbone's concerns and Alex's inability to learn anything about his background, Emma felt the man's magnetism. His casual yet commanding presence held everyone's attention.

"I'm not going to take much of your time tonight. I know you're eager to hear our fine barbershop quartet and shake a leg line dancing. Work off a few calories." He paused for more laughter. "But I just wanted to let you fine folks in on something exciting, on the big plans we have for our latest project." At his nod, Bill scurried forward and handed Marc a piece of glossy paper. "Many of you have heard of Tombstone, one of the most popular tourist attractions in the state. How would you like to have your own little Tombstone right here outside Sedona?"

This got laughs mingled with hoots at the pun.

"Well, we're going to build one. Right in the little old ghost town of Quincy."

Bill handed a stack of brochures to someone, and the pile began to make its way around the circle. Emma took one, holding it in the glow of the dancing firelight to read it. The main illustration was a map of the town, with existing and proposed attractions and activities labeled in different colors. Also to be built were condos, a huge hotel, an eighteen-hole golf course, and shops.

"This will cost millions," Emma whispered to Kelly as Marc continued rhapsodizing about Quincy's development and the benefits it would bring to the area.

"Lots of them," Kelly concurred. "I wonder where he's getting the financing. This type of development seems quite risky. What if they build it and no one comes?"

He finally closed with an invitation to visit the old mining town and see what they had done to date. He also invited anyone interested in learning more about the "opportunity," to seek him out.

To Emma's surprise, she saw Bev—the wife of a Lone Star Warbler they had met on the ruins tour—approach Marc. Several others followed suit. The rest of the crowd settled back and listened as the barbershop quartet started their set. Tonight they began with the Gene Autry classic, *Back in the Saddle Again*, embellished with percussion that sounded like hoof beats and a jingling horse's harness.

"I think I prefer the Aerosmith cover," Kelly whispered.

Emma gave her an elbow. "Shush. Admit it, this version is more appropriate." As though to underscore her words, the cattle in a nearby pasture began to bellow a chorus of moos.

After the quartet finished their last song, *Home on the Range*, Bill announced that the line dancing would begin shortly. Dakota had changed out of the Native American garb back into street clothes and joined them. The foursome made their way to the large barn. The huge double doors, at least twenty feet tall, were pushed back to their limits. Electric lanterns hung from ropes strung across the vast space, illuminating the worn boards of the dance floor and groupings of small tables on the sides. At the far end below the loft, the five-piece band was setting up instruments on a low stage.

The lead guitarist spoke into the microphone. "Good evening, folks. We're Honky-Tonk Rodeo Show." The drummer played a ruffle, and the rest of the band nodded and smiled while the audience clapped. "We live down the road a piece in Phoenix, and we're always happy to make the trip up here to the Double M. Beautiful country. Tonight we'll be playing a mix of line and partner dance favorites for all skill levels. For those of you new to line dancing, we're going to start off with a simple dance called Cowgirl Twist and Shout. Our in-house dancing expert Melanie is going to lead, so shake a leg and get out on the floor!"

The woman who had given them riding lessons moved to the center of the floor, clapping her hands. "Line up, everyone."

Kelly tugged on Emma's arm. "Let's go."

Emma dug in her heels. "I don't know if I want to." Although she enjoyed exercise in general, she was hopeless at structured dance, finding herself always zigging while the rest of the participants zagged. Her long arms and legs were always a beat behind.

"Why on earth not, Emma Jane?" Dottie Faye said. "There are all kinds of handsome cowboys here tonight. I can see at least half a dozen from here."

Indeed, among the people filtering into the barn were a variety of young men of all heights and hair and eye colors, their only common denominator was the ubiquitous uniform of cowboy hat, jeans, and boots.

"You don't partner with men in the line dance," Emma argued. She tapped her brim as a man wearing a particularly tall hat sauntered by. "And tell me, why are these things called ten-gallon hats anyway? They certainly wouldn't hold ten gallons of water, not even that goofy-looking one that guy's wearing."

"Or ten gallons of whiskey," Kelly quipped. "Or beer."

"Actually, ten-gallon is a misnomer," Dakota said. "The original word is Spanish, *galón*, and it refers to the braided hatbands *vaqueros* wore on their hats. Some wore ten, hence ten *galón*."

"Thanks for clearing that up," Emma said. "Now I won't picture them being used at the water hole."

Dottie Faye brought the conversation back to more important matters. "If I was a young woman needing to meet a man, how I'd go about it is I'd line myself up next to one of those ravishing young men. Then when the partnered dancing started, I'd conveniently be right there when he was looking around."

"That's crafty," Dakota said. "I'm definitely coming to you for dating advice, Dottie Faye."

Dottie Faye turned to Dakota and studied her speculatively, one dainty finger tapping her lips. "Hmm. You've certainly got a lot to work with, sugar. I've never seen such beautiful hair."

"Please don't encourage her," Emma said with a laugh. "She's a real schemer. She's been trying to marry me off ever since she moved to Mystic Harbor."

"I declare, Emma Jane, you're as obstinate as a mule," Dottie Faye protested. Her gaze from under thick lashes was sly. "I'm just trying to offer love a helping hand."

"I know you mean well, Aunt Dottie." Emma called her that to get her goat. "Sometimes love just needs a break."

"Last call for the Cowgirl Twist and Shout," Melanie shouted. The band struck the opening notes of Vince Gill's song *What the Cowgirls Do*. Kelly tugged Emma's arm again.

"Think of it as exercise. Come on." This time Emma let Kelly pull her onto the dance floor. At least she'd be out of reach of Dottie Faye's maneuverings for a while.

Kelly parked her between two cowboys before darting to the other side of one, Emma noticed with a wry grin. Oh, well. She ignored their existence and the occasional whiffs of men's cologne drifting her way, concentrating instead on following the instructor's directions. Stomp, stomp backwards then forward. Pivot. Twist, twist, twist to the left; twist, twist, twist to the right. Pivot the other direction. Kick and stomp backwards again, one, two. The moves were simple and slow, so for once, Emma didn't feel like she was making a fool of herself. She even found herself laughing and exchanging friendly smiles with her neighbors. After the song ended, she and Kelly stayed on the floor, joined by Dakota and Dottie Faye for the next few beginner dances, including the Cut a Rug and Country Slide. Dottie Faye especially was spectacular as she strutted her stuff up and down the floor, putting a little extra oomph in her wiggle.

The band took a brief break and Emma, her friends, and the nearby cowboys ended up standing in a circle waiting for the music to start up again. The tallest cowboy tipped his hat to Dottie Faye. "Ma'am, that was some serious rug-cutting you were doing," he said with admiration.

Dottie Faye swelled with satisfaction, patting her hair back into place. "Why, thank you very kindly, young man. I used to work as a dancer in my younger days."

Emma and Kelly exchanged amused looks. Yet another position the versatile Dottie Faye had held.

"I can believe that," he replied. He passed a glance around the circle. "All you ladies did a great job. Your first time line dancing, I gather?"

Emma laughed. "Yes. As I'm sure you could tell."

"Aw, shucks, not after the first number," the second cowboy said. He was shorter but good-looking in a pleasant boy-next-door way.

"Maybe you'd like to give the partner dances a try," the third, dark and lean, suggested. "They'll be doing those next set."

As Emma feared, her aunt's eyes lit up. *What the heck?* She was having much more fun than she had expected.

"Partner dances?" Dottie Faye said. "That sounds fun." She went on to introduce herself and the others. The men reciprocated—Slim was the tall one; the boyish one was Jim; and the dark one, Pete. Dottie Faye was almost beside herself with excitement when she realized that Pete was from "the civilized neck of the woods," Alabama, and Jim hailed from nearby Mississippi. "I'm in heaven," she declared. "Southern gentleman who are also cowboys. My, my." The men took her over-the-top flattery rather well, Emma thought. They didn't run away screaming at least.

The band returned to the stage, and this time Bill walked out onto the floor and announced he'd be calling the partner dances. "The Texas Two-Step," he bellowed. "Gentlemen, find your partners." The three cowboys each chose one of the younger women, and an older man standing nearby swept Dottie Faye off with a flourish. The two-step was simple, mainly a series of promenades and twirls as they moved around the floor to a sprightly tune. Then Bill called, "Change partners," and they did. By the time the dance ended, Emma had spun around in the arms of more men than she cared to think about. Young, old, fat, thin, handsome, not so good-looking—but all had treated her like a precious china doll as they guided her steps.

The three women were taking a break and drinking welcome cups of water when Emma spotted a familiar face across the barn, standing with a cup of soda in his hand. Dakota was talking to other acquaintances near the refreshment table.

"Well, lookee there," she said to Kelly, giving her a nudge. "Buck Rodgers. What a surprise."

"You really think he might be up to something?" Kelly said. Dottie Faye moved closer to hear what they were saying.

Emma nodded. "It's just a feeling I have. I can't believe it's a coincidence that he shows up everywhere we go."

"There's only one way to know," Dottie Faye said. "You need to dance him into submission and find out."

"OK," Emma said slowly. "How on earth can I pull that off?"

"I'll tell you." Dottie Faye gestured for them to move closer. "I've got a plan. And don't worry, sweet pea, we'll be your backup."

fifteen

Emma put a big smile on her face, grinning so hard that the corners of her mouth hurt. One, two, three ... she two-stepped around the room, made a twirl, then at the change partners signal, held her hand out to Buck Rodgers, standing on the sidelines. With a start of surprise, he put the cup down and took her hand, joining her in the circle of swirling couples. Her abandoned partner looked lost for a moment, then followed Emma's lead and brought Dakota onto the floor from her spot near the refreshments.

To Emma's delight, she realized Dottie Faye was right—a man couldn't resist an attractive smiling woman, and if she were determined enough, he would do whatever she asked. Not that she would ever apply this wisdom to her actual dating life. It was strictly for investigative purposes.

As they began to promenade, one of Buck's arms behind her shoulder, hands clasping, she noticed a wary but hopeful look in his eyes, like that of a mouse beguiled by a cat he hopes has good intentions. She also noticed his warm hands were much smoother than any self-respecting cowboy would sport. Although fit—his dance moves were surprisingly sprightly—he must work in an office. Another clue to Buck's real identity.

Circling the room, she kept an eye on Kelly and Dottie Faye. After they had slipped out of the barn's side door, she gave them a moment to get into place. "Phew!" she said, hoping to sound natural. "I'm feeling kind of warm." She twirled under his arm and back. "Do you mind if we get some air?" She nodded her head toward the nearby door.

"Not at all," he said gallantly. Ushering her with a protective arm, he guided her off the floor and outside. The light over the door illuminated only a short distance into the yard, and outside its circle, Emma saw a corral fence, shadowy horses moving and snorting in the darkness. She moved to the right of the doorway, onto the dirt. Where were Kelly and Dottie Faye? Something moved in the darkness, and she spotted them hovering on the other side of the entrance behind a lattice enclosure that, judging by the odors emanating from it, served to store garbage cans. Emma made sure she was turned toward them, ensuring that Buck would be facing the opposite direction of her covert companions.

"That was fun," Buck said. "I haven't danced in ages." He laughed, flapping his shirt away from his chest. "Good exercise too."

As his coat shifted, Emma noticed a bulge on his side beneath his arm. She had seen enough television shows and movies to recognize the object at a glance. Buck was carrying a concealed weapon under that innocuous-looking suit coat of his.

Her breath stalled as she pondered that fact. She knew that Arizona didn't require a concealed carry weapon permit, so even an innocent ranch-visiting tourist could be armed. Out West, it wasn't like only criminals and law enforcement carried a gun. But that scenario didn't seem to fit a line dancing event. Finally she choked out a response. "Uh, yeah. Even if you run, I guess it uses different muscles." Gosh, how lame. Emma was equally bad at subterfuge and flirting.

"You're right," Buck agreed.

Both of them fell silent, and every second of silence felt

like at least a minute. *This must be how a comedian who bombs on stage feels,* Emma thought.

The sound of a pebble hitting the fence got her attention. Making sure Buck wasn't looking, she glanced toward Dottie Faye, who had her whole head thrust out from behind the lattice. She gave the universal signal for "say something" and patted the air like she was touching someone. Emma put her hand on Buck's arm. He jumped, startled at her unexpected touch. "Buck," she said, inserting a warm note into her voice, "thanks again for saving me from that snake. I was really scared."

He ducked his head, kicking at the dirt with the pointed toe of his boot. "It wasn't anything. Just plain old common sense to avoid the thing."

"Yes, but so many people don't have common sense. Right?" She glanced at Dottie Faye, who gave her the thumbs-up.

He chuckled. "That's true, yes, ma'am, it is."

"So, what do you think of Sedona? We're just having a grand time on our vacation!" She laughed brightly, a sound that rang horribly false in her own ears.

He didn't seem to notice and gave her a smile in return. "Are you? That's nice."

"I remember you saying you were here on business. How's that going?" She gave another inane giggle. "Not that I'm trying to pry." *Yes, I am.*

"Business is boring and something best not discussed on a beautiful night like this, don't you agree?" He tipped his head back. "You can see so many stars out here in the West."

"That's true. I was noticing them myself earlier." For another seemingly endless moment, the two of them stood and gazed at the sky, listened to cattle moving around and the eerie howl of a coyote in the distance. Buck made restless movements with his feet and shifted his shoulders. Even Emma knew the universal signal of someone preparing to move on. She had learned exactly nothing. Desperately, she glanced toward Dottie Faye again for guidance.

Dottie Faye batted her eyes extravagantly and gave a horrible rictus grin. Obviously Emma needed to ramp up her flirting.

Emma detained Buck with another hand on his arm, rapidly batting her own admittedly less-than-lush lashes as she gazed up into his face. "Um, Buck ...."

"Yes, Emma?"

Taking a breath, Emma drew upon every memory of her aunt's skillful manhandling ability. Then, she was interrupted by a sound over where Dottie Faye and Kelly were standing. "Are you OK, ma'am?" a male voice boomed. "She's not having a stroke, is she?" was followed by Kelly's murmuring reassurances.

Emma couldn't allow anything to distract her from her mission. "Go on and admit it, Buck," she purred, lowering her voice to what she hoped was a sexy drawl. "You've been following me ever since we met at the airport. Well, now you've caught me." Emma almost threw up at her last words, but she steeled herself with the reminder that putting on an act, no matter how distasteful, was in a detective's job description.

Even in the dim light, she clearly saw the dumbfounded look on his face. "Listen, Emma. You're a pretty woman, but why on earth would you think I'm following you?"

"Maybe because you show up wherever I am. The resort, the gallery, and now here. Isn't that a wee bit strange?"

"It's all a coincidence, I promise." He shook his head. "I hope you're not spreading that rumor around."

Emma was stung. "Of course not! I don't need to pretend men are following me around to feel good about myself," she huffed.

"I wouldn't think so. Well, good night." With a tip of his hat, he disappeared into the night.

Emma stamped her foot and groaned. What a mess she'd made of things! Dottie Faye and Kelly hurried to her side. "What'd you find out?" Kelly asked.

"Well, I don't think he's on our trail. You should have seen his face when I suggested he was following me. I felt like one of those pathetic women who makes up romances."

"Don't feel bad," Kelly said. "A man thought Dottie Faye was having a stroke when she was coaching you." She hooted with laugher.

"Do you believe his nerve?" Dottie Faye grumbled. "Treating me like an old lady."

Emma had to laugh. "Oh, my. I was too focused on my fake flirting to really listen. Gosh, I'm bad at that stuff. I have new admiration for you, Dottie Faye. It's not easy being a man magnet."

Dottie Faye's expression cleared and she smiled. "How nice of you to say that." She took Emma's arm. "I can give you some more lessons, if you want. We'll get you paired up yet."

"That's OK, Dottie Faye. I don't think lessons will help. One more thing ...." She lowered her voice in case someone nearby was listening. "He was carrying a gun."

"So Mr. Rodgers is either a crook or a cop," Kelly said. "You must have gotten closer than you let on."

"We didn't get that close, but I thought the same thing." Emma desperately wanted to change the subject. "Is anyone else thirsty?"

"I am," Kelly said. "And those cookies looked pretty good too."

Rolling her eyes at Kelly's endless appetite, Emma led the way back into the barn. The band was taking a break, so they joined the swarms of people crowding around the refreshment table enjoying lemonade, water, and soft drinks. Bev and Stan, one of the barbershop quartet couples, joined them.

"How are you enjoying the ranch?" Bev asked.

"We love it," Emma replied. "Your performance was great," she said to Stan.

He smiled modestly, fingering his small beard. "We had a very good reception from this crowd, I must say. We'll be back again, I'm sure."

Bev nodded her head in excitement. "Especially since we're going to be involved in the Quincy development. We're getting in on the ground floor, aren't we, Stan?" She tucked her hand in the crook of his arm, her gaze fond and hopeful in equal measure.

He patted her hand and returned her smile. "It'll be a little tight, but I think we can swing putting in something. It's too good an opportunity to pass up. This area of the country is just exploding with tourism."

Foreboding ran up Emma's spine. The couple didn't seem like they were well-off enough to afford the gamble the development was sure to offer. Could the Quincy project be the business dealings John Longbone had been concerned about? Of course, promoting a risky investment opportunity wasn't necessarily illegal, even if it did skirt the edge of unethical. There had to be more to the story, but Emma felt certain the development was a critical piece of the puzzle of John's death.

"What's this?" Dottie Faye asked, quick on the uptake as

usual. Dottie Faye was nothing if not shrewd when it came to money and investments. Yes, her late husband, Archibald, had left her very comfortable, but that was decades ago. Dottie Faye had greatly enlarged her inheritance.

Bev explained the prospectus Marc was giving out to potential investors detailing the percent of ownership at different investment levels. "We can easily double or triple our money," Bev concluded.

Emma could tell by Dottie Faye's sour expression that she was deeply skeptical. But she didn't say anything. Instead she plastered a grin on her face. "That investment sounds right promising."

"Yes, Dottie Faye, I think you should look into it," Emma put in. Kelly gave her a puzzled look but then caught on to the ploy.

"There's Mr. Jacoby now," Bev said, waving to Marc as he crossed the dance floor nearby. Seeing her gesture, he changed direction and veered toward them. "I can introduce you."

"Oh, we've met," Dottie Faye said. "After I dropped a little pin money at his gallery."

"Mrs. Sinclair. Miss Cotton. Mrs. Grace. How nice to see you again." Marc was all smiles as he approached the group. "Are you enjoying our little shindig?"

"Absolutely. Everything has been so nice." Dottie Faye said, going into full-fledged Southern belle mode. "But I have to tell you, I'm real interested in hearing more about the Quincy project. Bev and Stan said it was looking like a surefire opportunity." She stared winsomely at Marc from under false lashes. "Daddy always told me to work with people you can trust. And with their recommendation, I feel comfortable enough to proceed."

Emma watched as Marc Jacoby's initial surprise was

followed by a smug smile. Greed—or something akin to it—flashed in his eyes. Apparently he thought he'd reeled in another gullible investor.

"But he also told me to be cautious," Dottie Faye added, wiping the smile off of Marc's face. "So you're going to have to do some convincing."

"I'd love to discuss the project with you," he said. "When would be a good time?"

"How about right now? Tomorrow morning we're heading to Quincy, and I'd like to get the lay of the land before we get there. Then I can picture what y'all are going to be doing."

"That makes sense," he said. "Come with me to the office. I'm sure Marge and Bill won't mind if we meet there."

Naturally, Emma and Kelly tagged along, which raised Marc's brows. "I don't invest in anything without letting my team look it over," Dottie Faye said, "They may look sweet, but they're as sharp as tacks when it comes to evaluating business deals."

Emma stood taller and put a serious expression on her face in an attempt to look like a business big shot, an effort almost derailed by Kelly's smirk.

Inside the office, Marc took off his cowboy hat, tossed it onto the desk, and indicated they should sit at the small meeting table in the corner. Picking up a silver metal briefcase, he unlocked it by rolling combination numbers. Emma had only seen a case like that in crime thriller movies, usually holding diamonds or cash.

"Ooh, keeping things under wraps, I see," Dottie Faye said.

No wonder Dakota didn't find anything in the gallery office. He keeps the important paperwork locked up.

"You can't be too careful," Marc replied. "There are a lot of people who would love to get their hands on this proposal.

There's a lot of proprietary and financial information in here." He pulled out three sheets of paper and slid them across the table, one to each of them. "Before I show you the prospectus, you have to sign this nondisclosure form." He handed around pens.

"Nondisclosure?" Kelly asked, tapping her pen on the table. "Which deal-points does it cover?" Emma stifled a laugh at her friend's business-speak.

"All of them. It means you won't reveal anything—not one word or number of what you're about to read—to any third party." His white teeth flashed in an unpleasant grin. "If you do, I'll have to kill you."

sixteen

"I'll have to kill you."

Emma's pulse raced as Marc's words sank in. Yes, she knew the phrase was an oft-quoted joke, but there was an edge to his voice she didn't like. This deal obviously meant a lot to him. Did it mean so much that he would literally kill to see it succeed? Had John Longbone gotten in the way? She glanced at the others to see their reactions. Dottie Faye slid her a tiny wink as she brushed a lock of hair out of her eye.

"My goodness, Mr. Jacoby, you can't mean that." Dottie Faye was a tall tower of outraged Southern womanhood, fit to be tied, as she often said. Glaring at Marc as though he were a lowly worm, she shoved back from the table and prepared to stand, obviously ready to walk out. "I am eminently trust-worthy. Ask my stockbrokers, bankers, and the trustees of my trust funds. I have several."

Lay it on thick, Dottie Faye! Emma and Kelly exchanged amused, triumphant glances and pushed back their chairs in imitation of the older woman.

Her reaction flustered Marc, and he hastened to reassure her. "Sorry, Mrs. Sinclair. Just a little joke. In bad taste, I admit. I didn't mean to offend you."

"Good. Now let's see that prospectus." Dottie Faye stepped up to the table again and signed the form with her big, flowery signature. Emma and Kelly did the same, although Emma had her fingers crossed under the table. If she found evidence of wrongdoing, she didn't care about any piece of paper she'd signed. The authorities were going to learn everything she knew.

Marc took their forms and countersigned. "I'd like one for my records too," Dottie Faye said. "An original." Marc tightened his lips but didn't say anything as he pulled out three more blank forms. They all signed again. Dottie Faye made a show of folding her form with perfect creases and tucking it in her handbag.

"Now let's see what you've got," Dottie Faye said, purely to unsettle Marc. It was a rare soul indeed who could suppress a reaction to Dottie Faye in full flirt mode. Flushing, he tugged at the collar of his Western shirt before pulling glossy bound booklets labeled "Quincy—Finding Gold in a Silver Mine," out of the briefcase and passing them around. The front photograph was a panorama shot of buildings arrayed on a hillside, mountains looming beyond.

Emma had no idea exactly what she was looking for, but she quickly leafed through the booklet hoping something would spark an idea regarding John Longbone's concerns about his business partner. Remembering that Alex Manning had found no trace of Marc's existence prior to his arrival in Sedona, Emma decided to start with the "About Us" section. Hoping to learn more, she flipped back to the index, found the page number, then turned to the right sheet.

A line of photographs were placed vertically—Bill and Marge Marshall followed by a Barbara Marshall—with biographies to the right of each grinning visage. "Where are you, Marc?" she asked, showing him the page. "Aren't you an owner?"

Marc grimaced. "I am, but my share is under my company. The Marshalls are the principals. Everyone else is a minority owner."

That's convenient. No need to explain who you are or reveal any past history.

"Your company? You mean the gallery?" Kelly asked.

"No. My other business. The Sedona Pottery Works."

Quincy was approached by a dirt road winding through the desert toward the mountains. "I'm glad a new road is part of the development plan," Kelly said as the convertible jounced over yet another section of corrugated road.

"It won't happen in time to help us," Emma said from her position behind the wheel, gripping it tightly as the car bounced and swayed. Dottie Faye was taking a break from driving, and she sat in the front passenger seat, regal in big sunglasses and a silk headscarf reminiscent of old-style movie stars of the 1950s.

"I just loved the expression on that scoundrel's face when I told him my attorneys would have to review the prospectus before I made a commitment," Dottie Faye said with a chuckle. "He was as nervous as cat in a room full of rocking chairs."

"Most people aren't savvy enough to get a lawyer's opinion, I'm guessing," Kelly said.

"Do you think Sedona Pottery Works is where you bought the bowl?" Emma asked Dottie Faye. "You did say it was a warehouse full of pottery."

"I can't say for certain since I didn't see a sign anywhere. And there wasn't one on the fence, remember?"

"It has to be connected," Kelly said. "John Longbone's bowl must have been sold to you by someone in business with Marc."

"We just need to prove it," Emma said. "Let's see if we can find a connection somewhere in Quincy."

"And now, ladies and gentlemen, we're approaching the eighteen-hole Quincy golf course," Kelly intoned as they passed through an area of dry, flat land marked only by a few pathetic shrubs, "famous for its sand traps." They all laughed. "And on the site of that mudhole over there," she added, a little further down the road, "you will soon see a swimming pool filled with sparkling blue water."

"You have a better imagination than I do," Emma said.

"Just mirages in the desert." Kelly referred to her brochure of the proposed resort. "According to this, the new condo hotel will be built right about here." They all looked at a wooden sign with a faded, peeling poster declaring Quincy, Arizona—The New Tombstone.

"I think he better allocate some money for new signs," Emma said. "That one doesn't exactly inspire confidence."

"I agree," Kelly said with a slight shudder. "There's something creepy about this place."

They arrived in what appeared to be Quincy proper, marked by dilapidated wooden buildings with collapsed roofs, some with trees growing right up through their middles. One was an elegant former train station, the tracks beside it pulled up long ago. They passed a house with curtains still hanging in an upstairs window, one stained white panel gently blowing out a broken pane.

"Do you think ghost towns have real ghosts?" Kelly asked rhetorically.

Emma groaned. "Please, Kelly. We have enough troubles without adding superstitious fears."

"The only ghosts around here are those of people's investment portfolios," Dottie Faye declared firmly.

"There's the Hotel Quincy," Emma said, spotting the sign on top of a square three-story building up ahead on the left. To both sides and across the street were rows of low storefronts reminiscent of a typical Western town seen in movies.

"This part's not so bad," Kelly said. "It looks like they've done some work here." Indeed, several of the buildings appeared to be freshly painted, and the porches and windows were all intact and in good trim. Only one store—the Quincy Trading Post—and a couple of restaurants appeared to be in use. "After we settle in, I want to go over to that trading post," Dottie Faye said as they all climbed out of the car.

"Good idea, Dottie Faye. You need one of those must-have animal skulls, perfect for all your Southwestern decorating needs," Kelly quipped, referring to the window display. "I see a buffalo, cattle head, and maybe a coyote. Can't tell from here." She went to the trunk and started unloading suitcases.

Joining her at the rear of the car, Emma shivered. "They're a little too authentic for my taste."

"Oh, come on, Emma. The buffalo will look splendid over your mantel." With a grunt, Kelly pulled out the last of Dottie Faye's luggage. She glanced at the hotel double doors, which stayed resolutely shut despite their arrival. "I'm guessing there's no valet service around here."

"I'll check," Dottie Faye said, sweeping into the hotel like the movie star she was imitating today. Emma and Kelly each picked up suitcases and carted them onto the low porch, at least getting them closer to the goal.

Dottie Faye burst back out through the doors, followed by an older man dressed like a janitor in blue work clothes. He even still held a wrench. "I can get those for you," he said, "although it's not really my job." He tucked the wrench in his back pocket and heaved up two of Dottie Faye's bags.

"Oh, are you the maintenance man?" Emma asked.

He chuckled. "Nope. I'm the plumber they brought in to fix the water pipes."

"Then we really can't ask you to carry our luggage!" Kelly protested.

"Oh, it's no trouble. I need a break to think on how I'm going to handle that maze of pipes going every which way down in the basement. What a cobbled-up mess that is." He gave Dottie Faye a warm, crooked-tooth smile. "I can't let a lady carry her own bags. Ain't fitting."

"Looks like Dottie Faye has created another admirer," Kelly said under her breath. "And I do hope that plumbing problem doesn't affect us." She and Emma grabbed their own suitcases and followed the pair inside.

"Where to?" the plumber asked once they entered the lobby, plainly furnished with a long front desk and several upholstered armchairs placed here and there near potted palms. Tucked in the corner was an actual brass spittoon, Emma realized with distaste. At the rear of the square room, a staircase ran up to a landing, made a right angle, and continued up. A cage elevator was chained and had an Out of Order sign.

Footsteps approached, and a middle-aged woman burst through the swinging doors at the back of the room. Emma recognized her as Barbara Marshall from the prospectus. Her face dropped when she saw the new arrivals. "Oh, I'm so sorry," she said. "You should have rung the bell." She pointed to the desk bell.

"I would have," Dottie Faye said, "but we just got here." The plumber was already sweating with the strain of carrying her heavy suitcases. "Before we do anything else," she added, "please tell us where to take our bags. The poor man's about to dislocate his arms."

With a start of surprise, Barbara noticed Dottie Faye was talking about her workman. "What are you doing?" she said to him. "I thought you were fixing the pipes."

"Just helping out," he replied stoically.

"I'm Dottie Faye Sinclair," she said helpfully, leaning on the desk. "We've reserved three rooms for tonight."

Barbara checked the computer. "You're in Room 4, Mrs. Sinclair." She pulled a key off the board and addressed the plumber. "That's at the top of the stairs. But please hurry. We need the water fixed so we can cook dinner."

Dottie Faye tucked the key along with a folded bill into the man's pocket, the one embroidered with "Conrad." Her pat on the shoulder seemed to revive him, and with slightly more energy, he trudged across the creaking floor to the staircase. "You'll have your water in a jiffy."

"We're with Dakota Longbone," Emma said to Barbara. "Is she here yet?" Dakota had left the ranch earlier that morning on business.

"She checked in just before lunch," Barbara said. "I think she's leading a horseback tour right now." She checked her computer. "You ladies are in rooms 5 and 6." She handed over two more keys with a laugh. "As you can see, the reservation system is up-to-date, but we're still using actual room keys. We're adding electronic locks as part of our improvement plan. And fixing the elevator, of course."

Conrad creaked back down the stairs, handed Dottie Faye her key with a salute to his cap brim, and disappeared through the swinging doors. Clanging and banging of pipes soon ensued.

"It's a quaint place," Emma said, casting an eye over the dark woodwork, gold-and-green wallpaper, and original light fixtures hanging from the beamed ceiling. "You wouldn't want to decorate it too modern."

Barbara warmed at this interest in her hotel. "You're absolutely right. All the renovations will be as unobtrusive as possible. Another thing we're doing is adding bathrooms upstairs. We'll have to give up a couple of rooms, but today's guests want their own bathrooms."

"We'd love to hear more about your plans," Kelly put in. "Mrs. Sinclair may become one of your investors."

If Barbara was friendly before, she positively glowed now. She scrambled around the corner of the desk and headed toward Dottie Faye, hand outstretched. "How wonderful to meet you." Her handshake was vigorous. "Before you head upstairs, let me show you around a little."

Emma and Kelly parked their suitcases, and the trio followed Barbara into the adjoining room, furnished as a parlor with upholstered furniture, a grand piano, and a fireplace decorated with the head of an elk hanging above. Some joker had rested a cowboy hat on the creature's antlers and stuck a cigar in his mouth.

"This is the old saloon, which was built by my ancestors right after the first Quincy silver strike in the mid-1800s. The original bar is still along this wall." To the left of the doorway, the elaborately carved mahogany bar had a brass rail, glass cabinets filled with bottles, and a wide mirror reflecting the room. "There's even a bullet hole." Barbara pointed out a deep dimple in one of the posts, and they all took turns feeling it. "Good thing Great-Grandpa ducked, or I wouldn't be here." She walked around to the back of the bar. "Can I get you something cold to drink? We've got iced tea, sparkling water, and soft drinks. Beer and wine too."

They decided on iced tea, and Barbara dumped ice cubes into glasses and poured tea from a container.

"A place this old must have lots of fascinating stories," Emma said.

Barbara slid three glasses across the bar, along with a dish of sugar and sweetener packets. A slice of lemon adorned each glass. "Have you heard about our ghosts?"

Kelly nudged Emma with a "what did I tell you" expression. "What's a self-respecting hotel without a ghost or two?"

"I'd say it's almost required," Dottie Faye put in, picking up three packets of sugar and shaking them. She tore the tops and poured a stream of white crystals into her glass.

The innkeeper added sugar to her own tea and stirred. "Well, if you've got time ...."

Her audience nodded, each leaning comfortably against the bar, with one foot up on the rail that had supported so many others seeking refreshment for more than a century.

"Remember that bullet hole? The night that happened, Great-Grandpa was tending bar. Quincy was pretty rough then, just a mining village full of hardworking, hard-drinking men and very few women. And the women that were here—well, they weren't exactly churchgoing schoolmarms, if you know what I mean. Great-Grandpa wasn't even married yet. He got hitched to his brother's sister-in-law the next year after she came to stay at the Double M Ranch." She opened a container of mixed pretzels, nuts, and cereal, poured it into a bowl, and set it on the bar.

"Yum. Thanks," Kelly said, digging her hand in for a scoop. "How'd you know?" She passed the snack bowl along to Emma.

"So brothers married sisters," Emma commented, selecting a small handful from the bowl.

"Like I said, there was a scarcity of women in these parts. But the Quincy Hotel did have a saloon girl, a beauty by the name of Arizona Alice. There's a picture of her right over there." The women trooped over to take a peek at a photograph of a pretty dark-haired girl hung next to the piano, right above that of a mustached man. "The bottom photo is my ancestor."

"Why didn't your great-grandfather marry her?" Kelly asked.

"Maybe she was a lady of the night," Dottie Faye suggested as they reassembled at the bar.

"She was rumored to be a 'soiled dove,' but we don't know for sure. We do know that she sang and played piano for the men and sometimes helped serve drinks. Many saloons hired women to entertain the customers, mainly to keep them drinking." She noticed Kelly's glass was almost empty. "Want a refill?" She topped off the glasses.

"Anyway, many men fell in love with Alice as you might expect, and no doubt Great-Grandpa had to step in now and again to keep his employee safe from their inebriated attentions. One night, things got out of control. The miners had just been paid, so they were bent on getting rid of the cash as fast as they could on drinks, card games, and raising heck. Things were in full swing when a certain cowboy arrived."

"Sounds like trouble," Kelly said, taking another handful of the crunchy treats.

"That's right. This particular cowboy had been courting Alice, serious-like. They were supposed to get married. Alice even had a wedding dress made. When the cowboy arrived, he wasn't too pleased to find her surrounded by drunk and lecherous miners. A gunfight broke out, and the cowboy and one miner were killed. Great-Grandpa was almost killed by that stray bullet." Barbara paused, letting the silence draw out.

"And Alice?" Emma prompted.

"Alice killed herself by jumping out her bedroom window." Barbara shook her head sadly. "And then Great-Grandpa got married," she added in a jovial tone, "and

Great-Grandma didn't allow any more saloon girls at the Quincy." She paused again for their laughter, and Emma sensed this was an oft-told tale.

"So who's the ghost?" Kelly inquired.

"All three." Barbara lowered her voice to a deep, mournful tone. "The rattle of the cowboy's spurs can be heard crossing this very floor. Some see the miner leaning on the bar, right where you two are standing." Emma and Kelly jumped. Barbara's voice became soft and dreamy. "And Alice? She wanders the halls, crying, a wraith wearing a white dress. The wedding gown she never got to wear, except in her casket. People have heard her footsteps. Sometimes they hear taps and bangs on the walls too."

"Oh, my," Dottie Faye said, a hand on her heart. "You tell that story so well."

"I guess it's in the blood. I come from a long line of barkeeps, and we're all about entertaining folks." Barbara took their empty glasses and wiped down the bar. "Now, if you're looking for something to do, there's a reenactment of another Quincy historic event in about an hour—a shoot-out between a gang of bank robbers and the sheriff and his deputies."

"That sounds fun," Emma said, "and we have time to go up and get settled first."

As they crossed the lobby, Dakota came in the front door. "Hey, ladies. I was hoping you made it." The four of them headed upstairs, and after washing up, they all convened in Emma's room.

"And I thought my room was small," Dottie Faye exclaimed, hands on her hips as she surveyed her niece's quarters. "There's barely room for the furniture in here." The room held a double bed, bureau, a nightstand, and a folding luggage rack. All four of them perched on the bed, as there wasn't anywhere else to sit.

"In the old days," Dakota said, "people didn't spend much time in their rooms. All the decorating money was spent on the public rooms."

"It's a good thing she gave you the largest room, Dottie Faye," Kelly said, "since you might become an investor." She winked.

Dakota's dark glance darted around the circle. "What's this? Fill me in. I'm sorry I was so tied up with tour business I couldn't help you investigate at the ranch. Apparently I missed something."

"You were asleep by the time we got in last night, and I didn't have the heart to wake you," Dottie Faye said. "I knew we'd see you today."

"Maybe it's a good thing you weren't around," Emma said. "You're a little too close to the players." She shared what they read in the prospectus during their meeting with Marc the night before. "So it looks like Marc is pulling the strings, but he's keeping a really low profile in the official documents."

Dottie Faye reached down for her bag and pulled her copy of the prospectus out. She flipped to the owner information page and handed it to Dakota. "See? He's not listed."

Dakota quickly scanned the page. "What does this mean?"

"We had our detective look into Marc's background, and he couldn't find any trace of him before his arrival in Sedona," Kelly said. "We thought it was suspicious."

"It sure is," Dakota agreed. "Especially since he showed up with a bunch of money to start the gallery."

Emma toyed with a loose thread in the chenille bedspread. "Marc said his investment in Quincy is channeled through the Sedona Pottery Works. Have you heard of it?"

Dakota shook her head. "That's not a retail store. I'm

very familiar with each and every one of those in town since I work closely with the owners in promoting them with the tour packages."

Emma and Kelly exchanged looks that said it was time to tell Dakota about the stolen bowl. "There's something else we need to tell you."

Fright flashed in Dakota's eyes. "What is it?"

Emma leaned forward and patted Dakota's arm. "It's not a matter of life and death or anything. We believe we have John's Anasazi bowl. It's in the safe at the resort."

"John's bowl? The one that was stolen during ...?" Dakota slid to the edge of the bed, looking like she was about ready to bolt.

"It's OK, Dakota," Kelly said, her voice soft and reassuring. "We got it by accident."

"I bought it from a low-down dirty crook," Dottie Faye said. "And I'm real sorry about that."

Dakota's mouth dropped as she realized the implications of what they were saying. "That means you know who killed John." She jumped up off the bed. "We need to go to the police. Right now."

"We will," Emma said. "I promise. But we want to know a little more first, so Dottie Faye won't be arrested for illegally purchasing a Native American artifact. You see, she didn't get a certificate of authenticity when she bought it. And she isn't entirely certain who sold it to her."

Dakota settled back on the bed while Dottie Faye explained how she was taken to the warehouse to buy the bowl. Emma and Kelly filled in the details on their attempts to trace the men, starting with the concierge, Percival, who quit the resort and moved away.

"So, when Marc said he owned the Sedona Pottery Works,"

Emma concluded, "I thought that might be where Dottie Faye bought the bowl. She said she saw shelves of pottery in the warehouse. If that's true, it gives us a direct link between Marc and the bowl."

"And between Marc and John's murder." Dakota bowed her head for a moment and when she looked back up at them, Emma saw the glimmer of tears in her eyes. "Good work, friends. Thank you so much—"

A loud creak sounded out in the hallway. Kelly burst off the bed and dashed to the door, opened it, and looked out. Shaking her head, she stepped back inside. "No one out there."

"Maybe it was one of the ghosts," Emma joked. "My money's on the cowboy. That creak was pretty loud."

"You mean the infamous Quincy Hotel ghosts?" Dakota said with a laugh.

"Yes. Barbara told us the story of Arizona Alice and the cowboy and miner who shot each other in the saloon. Alice threw herself out a window and now they all haunt the hotel." Kelly plopped back down on the bed. "I think it's just a ploy to drum up business."

"Probably so," Dakota agreed. "I've never seen or heard anything myself while staying here." She looked at her watch. "It's almost time for the reenactment. And after that, I'll go line up horses for our ride out to the mine tomorrow. How does that sound?"

Dottie Faye slid off the bed and stretched. She was wearing her belt-buckle cam with her blue jeans and Western shirt, Emma noticed. "Great. I'm going to do a little snooping after the shoot-out."

"Don't you mean shopping?" Kelly teased.

"That might be part of it," Dottie Faye acknowledged.

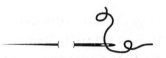

A festive air filled Quincy's streets as the reenactment got underway. Scattered among the throng of visitors were men and women dressed in costume, acting out roles as citizens of Quincy—shopping, sweeping the sidewalk, sitting and chewing the fat.

"This is cool," Kelly said as they found a spot to stand on the wooden sidewalk near the old bank building, which still bore faded lettering on the brick that read First National Bank of Quincy.

"The town looks totally different," Emma marveled. "When we got here, nobody was around."

Hoofbeats approached and six men, bandannas draped across their faces and guns drawn, thundered into town. They pulled up in front of the bank, their horses rearing and bucking. Two men stayed outside to keep watch while the other four went inside. Citizens scattered, calling the alarm, and one man was shot, falling flat right in the street.

"Did you see that?" Dottie Faye cried. "That dirty varmint." Those nearby smiled at her absorption in the show.

To cheers, the sheriff appeared on horseback, accompanied by several men. With a start of surprise, Emma recognized Buck Rodgers as the head lawman when he rode past, casting her a slant-eyed look of acknowledgment. Whether or not his role as sheriff was an example of typecasting remained to be seen, she thought wryly.

Buck and his deputies shot down the two bandits outside. As the other robbers emerged, bags of money in hand, a gunfight broke out. Besides the men in the street, men and even women stationed on roofs and balconies participated, acting on both sides of the law. Stunts, dramatic death throes, surprise twists, and pop-up participants (one out of a flour barrel) added greatly to the entertainment. The money sacks were passed along from hand to hand, even to audience members, who had to quickly get rid of the loot.

The show ended when two women dressed as saloon girls sneaked out of an alley, grabbed the money sacks and a pair of horses right from under the noses of the battling lawmen and bad guys, and to the laughs and cheers of the audience, rode out of town.

"That was really good," Emma said as they all applauded.

"A friend of mine wrote the script," Dakota said. "He did do a good job. Of course he did take a few creative liberties with the real story. And the performers do a lot of ad-libbing. It's different every time they do it."

"What fun," Kelly said. She asked Dakota another question about the choreography of the show, and the two of them began to chat.

Dottie Faye tugged at Emma's arm. "There he is." She pointed into the crowd of actors now walking up and down the dusty street.

"Who are you talking about? Buck?" The would-be sheriff was standing nearby in a group of admiring youngsters who wanted to handle his badge and six-shooters.

"No. Fiske. The driver who took me to the warehouse. He's wearing a red bandanna. Come on, let's follow him."

With a whisper to Kelly about what they were doing, Emma followed Dottie Faye into the street. They had to push their way through the crush—not an easy task—while keeping sight of the not-terribly-tall Fiske as he wove his way up the street. A block or two up, the crowd thinned and they realized he had slipped away.

"Dagnabbit," Dottie Faye said, stomping her cowboy boot. "The slippery little devil got away."

"At least we know he's in town," Emma pointed out. As they trudged back down the street, they spotted Kelly crossing toward them. Most of the visitors had left the street by now. Some could be seen entering the Quincy Trading Post, while others were seated inside the Country Kettle Café or the Silver Miner's Taproom. A small group trailed one of the saloon women as she gave a guided historical tour. At the end of the renovated blocks, Dakota could be seen entering the livery stable.

"What shall we do now?" Kelly asked, glancing longingly at the restaurant. "I smell french fries."

Emma checked her watch. "It's still a few hours until dinner at the hotel. We can go get a snack if you want."

"And then we can shop?" Dottie Faye demanded.

"Yes, Dottie Faye." Emma sighed. Between Kelly's bottomless appetite for snacks and Dottie Faye's insistence on buying shiny new things, she sometimes felt like she was accompanied by two children. Two very large children.

After bowls of bison chili and the requisite serving of piping hot fries for Kelly, the trio went across the street to the Quincy Trading Post. As might be expected, it was one of those establishments crowded with every last little item someone on the frontier, tamed as it might be now, might need or desire. Various sections held sporting goods, home furnishings, food, clothing, tack, and animal supplies. To add interest, antique items were used in displays. An old wagon held the store's selection of sleeping bags. Next to the barbecue grills and tools hung a rack of real branding irons. Rifles and bows and pickaxes and shovels decorated the walls and doorways.

To Kelly's delight, one area featured jars of penny candy and other packaged treats like canned rattlesnake, buzzard gizzards, and bison jerky. Dottie Faye lost herself in the footwear section, where she rapturously tried on numerous pairs of gorgeous hand-tooled boots in various heel heights. Emma, intent on continuing her sleuthing into Marc's companies, found her way to the gifts and souvenirs department. Emma was dazzled by the colorful array of cactus-, Arizona-, cowboy-, Native American-, and desert-themed items crammed onto the shelves.

Further along she came across a display of pottery in various shades of white and tan. She checked the bottom of a vase decorated with the ancient humpbacked flute player, Kokopelli. "Sedona Pottery Works" was stamped into the clay. Quite a number of pieces in the section were marked the same way.

Maybe Marc is legit after all. No, it's more likely this low-cost pottery is a front.

A young woman wearing a Quincy Trading Post apron like an old-fashioned shopkeeper came along the aisle. "Can I help you?"

Emma gestured at the shelves. "This is nice stuff, but I'm looking for something a little more high-end. Antiques if you have them."

"We absolutely do. Come this way." At the very end of the gift area, a long, glass-front case stood against the wall. The contents of the case were in another price bracket altogether. Emma whistled as she saw a display of pottery, baskets, arrowheads, and beadwork fit for a museum.

"Is there anything in particular you're looking for?" the clerk asked.

"No. I'm just browsing right now."

"I'll be over there pricing T-shirts if you need me to unlock the case."

Emma wasn't exactly sure what she was looking for, but she did know that it would take many trailer loads of cheap pottery to fund the Quincy project. There was also the fact that the FBI was involved. They only bothered with serious crimes. She walked back and forth in front of the case, allowing her eyes to absorb and enjoy the beauty and quality of the work.

Her late mother, Anna Belle Cotton, had enjoyed collecting antiques, and Emma had accompanied her on many buying trips to yard sales, stores, and auctions. Anna Belle studied collecting guides and history books in an effort to learn all she could. "It takes an eye to find the real bargains," she often said, "to spot the quality and authenticity no one else has noticed." Emma had watched her mother quickly scan a table full of items and pounce on the one that had any value. She also warned Emma about reproductions. "The more you know about materials, techniques, and the aging process, the easier it is to spot a copy," she had said.

In addition to whole pieces of pottery, the case held shards— scraps of broken pottery. Emma didn't see the appeal of collecting those, but they were relatively inexpensive except for some claiming to be prehistoric Hohokam. They were golden tan with figures and designs painted on them in pale orange. *Pretty.*

Something looked a little off about one near the back. It was slightly different in color, yet the design was exactly like one of the others. How likely was that? She was contemplating asking the clerk to open when the case when Kelly and Dottie Faye came rushing up. Kelly clutched a blue corn pancake mix with cactus syrup, and Dottie Faye was clomping along wearing mismatched boots of differing heel heights.

"Guess what?" Dottie Faye said in a loud attempt at a whisper. "He's here. Jim Smith. The man who sold me the bowl. I heard his li'l old squeaky voice in the back room."

seventeen

"**W**hat should we do?" Kelly said.

"I'm going in there," Dottie Faye declared, adjusting her belt. "I have my cam."

"You can't just barge in," Emma protested.

Dottie Faye clomped off. "Watch me. That slippery devil isn't getting away again." She quickly wiggled out of the store's boots and put her own matching pair back on.

Emma and Kelly followed her as she wove through the aisles to the shoe department. A half-open door opened into a stock room stacked with boxes of merchandise. "He's back there somewhere," Dottie Faye said. She pushed open the door, which plainly read Employees Only.

In single file they tiptoed through the storage area, pausing to listen every couple of feet. "You're right," Kelly said. "His voice really is distinctive." Through another partially open door came the rumble of male voices—or in Jim Smith's case, a high-pitched squeak.

"This is great," Emma whispered. "But remember to catch their faces this time." Another video with only voices, while helpful, would not be enough for them to take to the police.

"I've got it covered." Dottie Faye said. "Stand back." She eased the door open and entered, widening the opening just enough for Emma and Kelly to clearly see what was going on but not be spotted by those inside. The room was another stock area full of shelves and boxes. Jim Smith, Fiske (still in his red bandanna), and Marc Jacoby stood in the middle of the floor conferring.

Dottie Faye rested against the doorjamb, swaying slightly on her tall boots.

"Can I help you, Mrs. Sinclair?" Marc asked.

"I'm looking for the ladies' room," Dottie Faye claimed, taking several staggering steps along the concrete floor.

"I think it's out there to the left," Marc mentioned helpfully.

Not budging, Dottie Faye wiped a hand across her brow. "I'm not feeling very well," she muttered. She staggered forward again, triggering looks of alarm on the men's faces.

"Are you all right?" Marc exclaimed.

"Yes, ma'am, do you need a doctor?" Smith squeaked.

"Maybe ... maybe I do," Dottie Faye sighed. "I'm feeling kinda ..." She headed right for Smith, and as she reached him, she slung one arm around his bony shoulders and collapsed into his arms. "Faint."

Shorter than Dottie Faye and probably just over one hundred pounds soaking wet, Smith had trouble managing Dottie Faye's shapely but solid bulk. He staggered back toward the boxes, trying valiantly to either keep Dottie Faye propped up on her feet or lay her down gently on the floor. Emma had the fleeting vision of a lioness hurtling into the arms of a hyena.

"Whoa!" Smith cried as he and Dottie Faye slammed into the shelves. Boxes thumped to the ground with a bang, spilling out sweatshirts. Marc and Fiske had to jump aside or risk getting hit on the head. Smith's own boots clattering on the concrete like castanets, he wavered to one side and then the other, trying to control Dottie Faye's deadweight with his over-strained arms.

"Help me," he croaked, smothered by Dottie Faye as the law of gravity finally overcame his puny strength. He slid to the floor, lying sprawled with Dottie Faye across his chest. The other two men hovered over her, trying to pull her bulk off the smaller man. At first they worked at cross-purposes, with Marc pulling one way and Fiske the other.

"Pay attention," Marc snarled. Fiske, who never seemed to say anything, apparently functioned as some kind of low-ranking errand boy. Working together they rolled Dottie Faye off and laid her flat on her back.

Smith groaned. "I think I pulled something."

"We'll get to you in a minute." Marc shook Dottie Faye's shoulder, and her eyes flew open. "Mrs. Sinclair. Mrs. Sinclair."

She blinked thick lashes slowly. "Oh, did I pass out?"

"Yes, you did. Perhaps I should call a doctor."

Showing an amazing recovery, Dottie Faye sat right up. "Don't bother. It's my new medication. I need to drink more water. That's all. The doctor warned me I might get woozy."

"Fiske. Get the lady some water," Marc barked. As Fiske headed for the doorway, Kelly pulled on Emma's arm and the two of them hid behind a stack of boxes.

"That's one way to catch a bad guy. Squish him," Kelly teased. They were reviewing the video on the laptop in Dottie Faye's room before dinner.

Dottie Faye harrumphed. "It's not my fault he's a shrimp."

"At least you got their faces this time," Emma said. "They're clear even if the camera does swoop around a bit." Dottie Faye had caught Smith from several angles, and some of his expressions were downright comical. Later in the video, both Marc and Fiske could be seen leaning over Dottie Faye in concern.

"Perfect," Kelly said. "We can prove that Marc knows the guys who sold you John's bowl, Dottie Faye." She glanced at Dakota. "Are you doing OK with this?"

"To be honest, I'm overwhelmed," Dakota admitted. She bit her lip. "It's one thing to have a theory, but to find out that someone you trusted ..." Her voice trailed off. "I just don't know why Marc would do such a thing."

"I have an idea," Emma said solemnly. "But brace yourself. It's not pretty." She dug around in her handbag for the pottery shards she had purchased, both packaged in small plastic bags. She laid them on the bureau and waved for Dakota to take a look. "I bought these at the Quincy Trading Post today."

"Hohokam," Dakota said. She picked up one and studied it. "Unusual color and artwork. Nice." She picked up the second and did the same. Then something seemed to click, and she gave Emma a puzzled look.

Emma pulled out the magnifying glass she carried to examine textiles and stitching in quilts. "Let's look at them more closely." Emma had carried out this experiment earlier and knew what Dakota would find.

"This one's a fake," Dakota said with disgust. "The back side is too smooth, like it was machine made. Someone tried to make it look authentic, but the ridges go the wrong way." Anger flashed across her face as she read the little card purporting the piece as prehistoric Native American. "What does this mean?"

Emma took a breath, glancing at Kelly and Dottie Faye for reinforcement. They both nodded encouragement. "This might be a stretch, but I think Sedona Pottery Works is turning out fakes along with the tourist pottery. I didn't have a chance to look at everything in the case, but I wouldn't be surprised if some of the so-called antiques are actually fakes."

Dakota sank back down on the bed. "So you think Marc is turning out fake Native American pottery?"

"Yes," Emma said, pacing back and forth with agitation. "It's the only thing that makes sense. This afternoon I did some research online and found out there's a huge black market in forged Native American pottery. Because of the restrictions on sales, unscrupulous buyers often don't ask too many questions when it comes to the really valuable and rare pieces. And some of it is sold openly to people who don't know any better, slipped in among real stuff, like these shards."

"Sounds like what happens with art forgery," Dottie Faye commented. "I've heard of people copying a stolen painting and then selling the forgery. What's the buyer going to do? Complain to the police?"

"Assuming you're right, no wonder John was upset. The only thing worse than selling artifacts illegally is forging them." Dakota could barely get the words out, she was so visibly upset. Tears sprang to her eyes. "What a hypocrite! Pretending to support our work while all the time he's faking it for profit. I'd like to kill him!"

Kelly sat beside Dakota and put her arm around the other woman's slender shoulders. "Totally understandable. But we've got to stay calm and try to get some more information when we go out to the mine tomorrow. Then we'll go to the police."

"No," Emma said. "We'll go to the FBI. I think that's why Wayne Bryant was sniffing around. He's on the trail of the forgery ring." She smirked. "I can't wait to see his face when he learns we've solved his case for him."

"Emma Jane, I'm starting to wonder about your problem with authority," Dottie Faye scolded mildly.

Emma snorted. "It's not authority per se. It's arrogant law enforcement personnel who don't listen."

A reluctant smile broke across Dakota's face. "You guys crack me up." She glanced at her watch. "I think we have time before dinner to get a lay of the land."

Everyone agreed, and Dakota unfolded an official United States Geological Survey map of the Quincy area onto the bed. Wavy lines showed elevations of hills and rock formations. "This is the mine right here," she said, placing her finger on the spot. "This is the old road leading from town to the mine." She indicated the route, marked by double dotted lines. "It's not maintained anymore, so it's pretty rough for regular vehicles. I think we should go this way, along this trail." She traced a route through a canyon and around some rock formations. "It's longer, but we'll sneak up on the site without being seen."

"Where are the hazards?" Kelly asked.

Dakota showed them the relevant symbols. "If you avoid crossing the old tunnels or going near the shafts, there's absolutely no chance for an accident. Besides, there are signs you can't miss too. Marge was stating the case a little too strongly."

"To keep people away," Emma said. "More proof there is something going on."

"Is everyone clear on the route?" At their nods, Dakota folded the map. "I think we should head out pretty early. Right after breakfast."

"Sounds good," Dottie Faye said. "I'm eager to put this case to bed."

Kelly laughed. "You're starting to sound like a real detective, Dottie Faye."

"Speaking of detectives," Emma said, "ours struck out on

Hannah Beiler. Is there anything else you can tell us about her, Dakota?"

Dakota shrugged. "Like what? Her looks?"

"No, although a picture would be great. I don't suppose you have one?"

"No. We weren't that close."

Emma put the pottery shards back in their little bags. "I was thinking more about what she was like as a person, anyway. Did she have any hobbies or interests beyond the class? Like if someone was looking for me, it would be helpful to know I like to run and do yoga." At Dakota's silence, she added, "I know it's a long shot. Like you said, you barely knew her."

Dakota held up a hand. "Wait. I think there is something. Since we met at night, we got in the habit of taking turns bringing in snacks. Someone started it with a batch of brownies. I remember that Hannah brought in these awesome little cherry pies. Individual ones." She demonstrated by putting her fingers into a small circle. "Anyway, that was one of the best pie crusts I had ever eaten. It melted in my mouth."

"It must have been, if you remember it fifteen years later," Kelly said. "As a food lover, I can relate."

"Thanks, Dakota," Emma said. "Who knows, maybe she's famous for her baking by now."

"We'll have to eat our way across Amish country, following a trail of pie crumbs." Kelly didn't look exactly sad at the thought.

"Speaking of eating," Dottie Faye said, "the dining room should be open now."

Kelly bolted for the door. "Great. All this talk of pie is making me hungry."

In the hallway, Dakota hung back. "Please don't take offense," she said to their questioning looks, "but I really need to be alone right now." She put her hand to her midriff. "I don't have any appetite, either."

"We understand," Emma said. "Come find us later if you want to talk."

Dottie Faye locked the door, and as Dakota went down the hall to her own room, the trio headed for the stairs. "I don't blame her," Kelly said. "It's a pretty upsetting situation, and we gave her a lot to think about."

Emma could sympathize with the churning emotions that accompanied thinking about a loved one's murder. *How will it feel when I come face-to-face with Rose's murderer, the way Dakota has with the man responsible for her cousin's death?*

A creaking sound was heard from a dark corner just beyond the stairs. Kelly cast Emma a mischievous look. "Let's go." Followed by Emma and Dottie Faye, she continued down the hallway until they spotted what was making the eerie noise. A rocking chair was moving back and forth all by itself.

"Maybe someone was sitting there and they just got up," Emma suggested.

"It's probably the ghost of Arizona Alice taking a rest before the evening's work," Dottie Faye said, her eyes wide.

The rocker came to a stop and sat there innocently as Kelly felt around the floor. "I can't find any wires or anything." She jumped up and down on the floor, seeing if the boards were uneven enough to make the chair rock when someone passed nearby. But the chair remained unmoved by Kelly's exertions.

Emma had more important things on her mind than improbable ghosts. "Come on. Let's go eat. It's probably just a trick to make people think the place is haunted."

In bed later that night, Emma hoped that the strange noises she heard were either trickery or just the odd sounds that old buildings tended to make as they settled at night.

Even her sweet cottage back in Mystic Harbor could make mysterious creaks and groans, especially in the winter.

Footsteps tapped down the hall, but instead of the expected sound of a door opening and closing, she heard nothing. A series of bangs up and down the walls were next, followed by a wheezing sound, and a final punctuating boom. Perhaps it was the pipes; Emma's room was right beside the shared bath. *Air in the pipes made a lot of noise, right?*

The narrow bed was lumpy, and Emma hoped new mattresses were on the renovations list. She tossed and turned trying to get comfortable, wishing she was at home in her own bed. She hadn't gotten a good night's sleep yet. After a few days on the road, she longed to be back in familiar surroundings, working at the store and enjoying her perhaps unexciting but pleasant daily routine. She and Kelly were lucky in that they enjoyed their chosen profession so much it wasn't really like work at all.

Maybe it was good to go away. It made you appreciate your blessings that much more.

Footsteps sounded again, tapping lightly past her door. Emma tensed, debating whether or not to get up and see who was out there. Gripping the sheets with her fingers, she made herself stay in bed. Most likely it was just another guest going to his or her room. Or alternately, a recording of fake ghosts set to go off at intervals during the night. She pictured a tape player hidden somewhere in the hallway. Nowadays it would probably be a computer file, one of those MP3s. She was just drifting off, thinking nonsensically of how she would rig a place for ghost sounds, when something jarred her fully awake.

A muffled woman's scream. Emma sat up. Then, just as suddenly, the sound choked off.

She heard a loud thump, then silence.

eighteen

The hotel was so quiet after the scream that Emma told herself she must have imagined it. Maybe she had been asleep and dreaming, even though she had the perception of being awake. Dreams were strange that way. She had even dreamed she was dreaming once. Or maybe it had been the grand finale of the ghostly sound effects: the scream and thump of Arizona Alice's suicide as she jumped out the window.

That was a revolting thought.

She lay dozing in the uncomfortable bed, one ear cocked for any further sounds, but heard nothing until close to dawn when a nearby rooster crowed. Another sound effect to give the sense of being back in time, or were there really chickens nearby? Sitting up, she pulled the window shade. With a snap, it rolled up to the top of the window, revealing Quincy's main street. Nothing stirred out there except a stray dog nosing his way along the sidewalk. He disappeared into the alley beside the Country Kettle restaurant, no doubt searching for garbage to get into.

Everyone else was probably sleeping in, but Emma got up, propelled by the need to make sure everything was all right with her companions. She was also eager to go out to the mine and see if they could learn anything there. They had almost put all the pieces together, and they needed to move quickly before Marc and his cohorts caught on.

She quickly slipped into jeans and shirt but didn't bother with shoes. Instead, she padded out to the hall in her stocking feet. She stopped in the bathroom to wash her face and comb her hair, which showed the effects of her uneasy night in bed by sticking out every which way.

Dottie Faye didn't answer when Emma rapped lightly on the door. Putting her ear to the panel, she heard her aunt's telltale gentle snores. Dottie Faye was all right. Kelly's room was next to hers and again, she knocked softly. "Yes?" Kelly called out. She was a light sleeper, like most mothers.

"It's Emma. Just seeing who's up."

Kelly groaned. "Not me. Come back in an hour."

Emma moved along to Dakota's room, which was at the end of the hallway near the back stairs. At her first knock on the door, it swung inward.

Uh-oh. That wasn't right.

Emma pushed the door the rest of the way open. Dakota's bed was rumpled, the covers thrown back, as though she'd been sleeping but had gotten up.

Then Emma noticed the overturned straight-back chair next to the wall. Yes, Dakota could have knocked it over in her haste to leave, but it just didn't seem likely. Besides, where did she go? She wasn't in the bathroom, and the dining room wasn't open yet. Nothing in town appeared to be, either.

She remembered the scream and thump she had heard. Her blood iced. Dakota had left all right—against her will. They'd taken her down the back stairs, and that was why she hadn't heard them going by her door.

Pushing down her feelings of fear and dread, Emma stepped into the room. She had to see if there were any clues about what had happened here or where Dakota had been taken. Perhaps the kidnappers had conveniently left a clue to their identities—like a stray button or something lost out of a pocket. Emma had no doubt more than one person was involved. It would take someone awfully strong to overpower a woman like Dakota without help.

Unless drugs were used to knock her out. Feeling sick, Emma scanned the room. Most of Dakota's clothing was piled neatly in her suitcase, with a couple of discarded items placed nearby. Emma got down on her knees and pulled up the bedspread to look under the bed. Dakota's handbag was stuffed under there. She pulled it out and, steeling herself against a sense of intrusion into her friend's privacy, peeked inside. Dakota's wallet was there as was her cellphone. That clinched any idea that her departure was voluntary. No woman went anywhere without her wallet or cellphone. Or left her door wide open.

Emma continued her hands-and-knees search of the room but found nothing more than healthy dust bunnies way under the bed. Standing up, she scanned the bed, picking up the pillows. Under one pillow was the USGS map of Quincy. That was an odd place to find it, nowhere near the purse where Dakota had stowed it after their meeting. Maybe Dakota had been looking at it before bed, but surely she would have put it on the nightstand or the floor, not under her pillow. Was it a clue?

Maybe it was a stretch, but Emma decided she was going to take it as a message from Dakota. Someone had taken her to the mine.

She found the room key on the nightstand, grabbed Dakota's purse, hung the Do Not Disturb sign on the knob to keep hotel staff out of the room, and locked the door. If they couldn't find her quickly, they'd have to call in law enforcement. But it could take hours to get officers out to Quincy. The fake sheriff and his deputies didn't count. Besides, policemen had rules when adults disappeared, claiming that twenty-four hours were needed to consider someone missing.

She doubted they would consider a left-behind purse and an open door signs of foul play.

No, it was up to her, Kelly, and Dottie Faye to find Dakota before it was too late.

She stowed Dakota's purse in her suitcase and locked it, and then she went to wake the others. Her discreet "Houston, we have a problem," was enough to rouse Kelly out of bed.

"What's up?" she asked, yawning as she opened the door. Emma filled her in. "I'll get dressed," Kelly said. "Then how about I go down and see if I can get us coffees and something to go? We're going to need nourishment."

Emma went along to Dottie Faye's room to rouse her and then finished getting ready in her room, putting on her cowboy hat, boots, and jacket. The desert was cold in the morning.

After Kelly returned with sacks of food, they went to Dottie Faye's room to collect her. "Come in," she called at their knock. They entered to see her fastening a belt holding a pair of six-shooters around her waist.

"Dottie Faye. You didn't bring those from home, did you?" Emma was appalled at the idea that Dottie Faye had packed firearms in her suitcase.

"Don't go off half-cocked, Emma Jane," Dottie Faye joked, making a pun with one of her favorite Southern sayings. "These are replicas. I bought them at the Quincy Trading Post after supper." She settled her cowboy hat on her head. "But I am wearing some real spy equipment." She slipped into her fringed jacket. "You'll find I'm well-prepared for our mission."

"Should you choose to accept it," Kelly quipped. She brandished the bags. "I'm well-prepared too. Coffee plus egg-and-cheese biscuits. Those will keep us going."

"I'll grab bottles of water," Emma said.

They nibbled on the biscuits and drank coffee as they

walked over to the livery stable. "Uh-huh," Kelly said, cramming the last of the rich, warm sandwich into her mouth. "One thousand calories of pure pleasure."

Inside the stable, they found the sleepy attendant forking hay into the horses' stalls. "Have you seen Dakota Longbone?" Emma asked with the hope that her friend might have left the hotel under her own steam.

He leaned on his pitchfork, scratching his thatch of blond hair. "I haven't seen her since yesterday," he said, "when she booked four horses for today."

Kelly jabbed a thumb at her chest. "That's us. Well, three of us."

"I guess we won't need the fourth horse," Emma said.

"Just give me a few minutes. I'll get them saddled up for you," he said. They perched on a stack of hay bales and sipped their coffee while waiting.

"Where you headed?" he asked casually, holding the bridle of Emma's horse as she mounted.

"Oh, just out for a ride in the desert," Emma said.

"Don't get lost," he warned. "There's an old mine out there."

"We've got a map," Dottie Faye said breezily, climbing aboard her own horse, a tall bay.

"She booked you for a half day, but as long as you're back by noon, you should be good. I won't charge you for the extra hour."

"Thanks," Kelly said, giving her horse an experimental little kick with her heels so he'd start moving. The pinto took off at a trot.

"Watch out for that one," the attendant called. "He's a tad frisky."

Kelly held on to her hat, pulling back on the reins with the other hand. "I see that," she yelled. She slowed the horse to a walk, and the other two caught up. "Which way do we go?"

Emma studied the map. "We go all the way through town and then turn left onto the trail." They rode three abreast right down the middle of the road, still the only people out and about. Emma fancied she was experiencing Quincy the way it was a century ago, before the automobile transformed transportation forever.

Clouds touched with salmon and purple drifted in the endless sky, and the misty blues and lavenders of the desert landscape slowly transformed into gold as the sun edged above the horizon.

"This is downright amazing," Dottie Faye said, gazing around in wonder.

"The sunrise?" Kelly replied. "Yes, it is."

"I mean that I'm up to see it. Now I know what all the fuss is about."

"I wish we were enjoying it under better circumstances," Emma said through tight lips. She urged her horse to move faster as they left the road and entered the trail, marked by a pile of stacked stones.

For a while they headed out into what looked like desert wasteland, wandering through shrubby hills and flat tracts marked only by clusters of cacti. Finally, off in the distance, they spotted the unusual rock formations they'd seen in the mine photographs.

"Stop," Emma called. "I need to check the map." Tracing her finger along the trail, she tried to estimate where they were by how long they had been traveling. They were supposed to approach the rock formations from the north, but they were now approaching them from the west. Sweat trickled down her back as she realized she must have gotten off the trail somehow.

"Is something wrong?" Kelly asked, always quick to pick up on Emma's distress.

In response, Emma slid down from her horse and gestured for the other two to do the same. After they clustered around, she pointed out where she thought they were relative to the rocks near the mine versus where the trail would have put them.

"I think I missed one of the markers," she said. "Or I mistook random rocks for a marker."

Kelly studied the desert, her face serious under the brim of her cowboy hat. "I don't think we should try to find the trail again. Why don't we just head for the formation directly?"

Emma studied the terrain markings on the map. "It doesn't look like we're going to have to cross any canyons or anything. But we will be going awfully close to the mine itself. Are you OK with that?"

"We've got to get Dakota out of there," Dottie Faye said. "And they always say a straight line is the shortest distance between two points." A crow cawed overhead. "He agrees with me. It's not too far, as the crow flies."

"All right," Emma said. "We'll do it."

They climbed back on the horses and set out across the landscape. In the lead, Emma did her best to spot any hazards and adjust their course to go around them. At one point they had to skirt a wide area of cacti and other prickly desert plants. A dry wash posed a challenge since the steep banks were loose with soil and rocks, dangerous for the horses. They were forced to go downstream a distance to find a natural crossing place.

Dottie Faye averted disaster with quick work on the reins, making her horse dance and prance and rear up as she backed away from a sinkhole above a mine tunnel, marked only by a cluster of bushes and a few pieces of wood fence collapsed into a heap. "That one wasn't on the map!" Emma cried, her heart thumping in panic.

"Don't pitch a conniption over it, Emma Jane," Dottie Faye soothed, patting her horse's neck to settle her down too. "We're all right. And we're almost there."

The formation was straight ahead, thrusting out of the flat ground like skyscrapers on a city street.

They tied the horses in a sheltered spot under an outcrop so they could approach the mine building on foot. Working their way through the rocks, they soon found themselves gazing down from an outcrop at the tumbledown stone building with its rusty metal roof. On the quiet desert air, they clearly heard the hum of equipment emanating from the building. As they watched, a truck approached down the old road, kicking up dust.

"There's Marc's Jeep," Emma said, pointing to a white Cherokee parked next to other vehicles in an uneven line next to the building.

"I didn't know he had a Jeep," Kelly said.

Emma shrugged. "I saw him get out of it in the ranch parking lot when we first got there. I guess I noticed since I drive one too. His is newer, of course."

"Here," Dottie Faye said, handing Emma a pair of small binoculars.

"Where are you going?" Kelly called as Dottie Faye started to pick her way through the rocks.

"I'm going to reconnoiter a bit."

"I think she just likes that word," Kelly said to Emma after Dottie Faye's departure.

Emma trained her binoculars on the approaching truck. It pulled up behind the building and backed into a loading bay. A wide metal door opened with a screech. The driver, a burly man rather tall, got out and opened the rear of the truck. A second thinner man joined him.

"They're bringing out pallets," Emma said. She zoomed in. "Cardboard boxes."

"That's pretty boring." Kelly looked around. "Where did Dottie Faye get to?"

Just then the older woman's voice rang out clearly. "Put your hands up."

nineteen

Emma and Kelly exchanged alarmed looks.

"What is she up to now?" Emma exclaimed. It was a pretty risky move for Dottie Faye to try to arrest someone with toy guns.

Leaving their observation perch, they clattered back through the rocks to where Dottie Faye stood, her gun pointed at Buck Rodgers. His eyes widened when he saw the other two approaching. "Tell her I'm a good guy," he called.

Dottie Faye waved the gun. "And I'm Mae West. Keep your hands up where I can see them. And away from that gun under your jacket."

His face was almost comically startled. "How'd you know—?"

"We know everything," Dottie Faye snarled.

He tried again. "I'm an FBI agent. I can prove it."

An awful thought stopped Emma in her tracks. Could it be? "Are you Wayne Bryant?" If he were the agent who had talked to John Longbone, then so much would make sense. The way he seemed to be following them—he'd really been following the same trail of clues and connections.

He seized on her words like a lifeline. "That's right. I'm Wayne Bryant. I've been working undercover."

"You're just saying that," Dottie Faye said, waving the gun again.

The man cringed. "Please, ma'am. That thing could go off."

Not likely. "Lie down," Emma ordered. "If you're Wayne Bryant, you'll have ID."

Buck or Wayne or whoever he was awkwardly dropped to his knees and lay facedown flat in the dirt. Emma and Kelly scurried over. "My badge is in my coat," he said. Squeamishly, Emma pulled it away from his body and reached inside the jacket's top inside pocket. Yes, there was a leather case in there. She pulled it out and flipped it open. Badge and picture ID. "He's FBI, all right," she said. "You can get up now. Stand down, Dottie Faye." Her aunt reluctantly holstered her gun.

Kelly cast a raised brow her way. "You sound like an actor in a movie."

Emma shrugged. Maybe it was the cowgirl outfit, but for some reason she felt completely in character as a take-no-prisoners investigator. Buck, really Wayne, pushed himself to a standing position and dusted off his knees. "So, Wayne, I take it you're on the trail of the pottery forgery ring too?"

Now he raised his brows high. "Too? What are you women doing investigating a federal crime?"

"Actually, we were investigating a murder, but we stumbled across the forgery ring. That's the motive for John Longbone's murder, right? He threatened to blow the whistle on Marc Jacoby?"

"I don't know if I should be talking about this with you."

"So you said during our phone call a couple of days ago." Wayne nodded as he put two and two together. "But we've got information for you, and if you want to hear it, you'll cooperate."

"What information?"

Emma made a "come on" gesture. "Just confirm our theory, please. Then we'll spill."

Wayne sighed. "Yes, we've been investigating the pottery ring for a while. We traced it back here to Sedona and Marc Jacoby."

"And Marc Jacoby is an assumed name, right?"

"How do you know that?"

"We have our own sources," Emma said.

"So then you know he's really a low-level money launderer for organized crime back East. He took a bunch of their dough and skipped town, tried to reinvent himself as a legitimate businessman."

"Is that what John Longbone figured out? That his partner was a crook?'

"I'm not certain. He did find out about the pottery ring, and he wanted to help us infiltrate the gang. Then he was murdered. The story that it was a robbery gone wrong was something we concocted so the criminals wouldn't realize how close we were."

"I have a piece of evidence for you," Dottie Faye said. "By accident I bought John Longbone's Anasazi bowl—the one that was stolen from his house that night." Her face was pained. "I'll turn it in any time you want."

"She didn't know any better," Kelly said hastily. "And we have video proving that Jim Smith, the man who sold her the bowl, and Marc Jacoby are connected."

A surprised expression flashed across his face, but he merely said, "Good work. Now what brings you out here?"

Emma pointed at the stone building. "Dakota Longbone has been kidnapped, and we think she's in there." The driver had finished unloading the truck and was now driving away in a cloud of dust. The metal door to the warehouse clanged shut.

Wayne whistled. "Kidnapped? Tell me more." Emma quickly filled him in on Dakota's disappearance from her room. "I suppose she could be somewhere else, but Marc Jacoby's here. So I think she is too."

The federal agent dug in his pocket and pulled out his cellphone. "That changes everything. I was here on reconnaissance, but now it's a rescue mission. I'm calling for backup." He frowned as the phone powered up. "Darn. Not a single bar." He waved the phone in the air, stood on a rock, and went through other gyrations in an effort to pick up a signal. Emma and Kelly checked theirs too, with the same result.

Dottie Faye took off her boot and held it out to Wayne. "Try this."

"What the heck?" He stared at Dottie Faye as if she were insane.

She waved the boot at him. "It's a satellite phone. You ought to think about getting one for yourself." He skeptically took the boot and followed Dottie Faye's instructions on how to access the phone under the heel. Politely, the trio moved aside as he made the call. "Yes, Boss," they heard him say, "I'm calling from the site. No, not on my phone. You wouldn't believe it if I told you."

Emma smiled, wondering if Wayne felt like the agent from *Get Smart* who had a shoe phone.

He disconnected and handed the boot back to Dottie Faye. "A SWAT team will be here shortly. Air and ground teams both."

Hitching up his belt, he turned and started to pick his way through the rocks down the slope toward the building. "Where are you going?" Dottie Faye demanded, her boot still half-off.

"You ladies stay here. I'm going to go get the lay of the land for the team."

"Not without us," Dottie Faye cried, cramming her foot in the rest of the way. "Besides, you might need my boot again."

"All right," Wayne snarled. "But stay back, and don't get your heads blown off. I don't feel like filling out the paperwork."

"Touchy, touchy," Dottie Faye said. "Someone that ornery must be a Yankee."

The four of them picked their way through the rocks and bushes, careful to keep low to the ground so they wouldn't be visible should anyone be looking from the old stone building. There weren't any windows on the side, so Emma felt pretty confident that their approach had been unnoticed.

About halfway down the length of the building, another wide door stood open, and they glimpsed a workman loading unfired pottery into a huge brick kiln. Emma realized that, in the desert climate, the temperatures in the building must be unbearable once the kiln was operating. Perhaps they worked at night, when temperatures were cooler.

The workman glanced right toward them, and they all quickly ducked behind the rocks. Had he spotted them? Would the next thing they heard be his cry of alarm?

When Emma finally braved a look, she saw the workman pull out a pack of cigarettes and light one up. They had to crouch for a good five minutes without moving a muscle, knees and backs protesting, until the man threw his spent cigarette butt on the ground and went back inside.

Once he was out of view, they quickly scurried along a windowless, doorless section of the long building that appeared to be a series of sheds. As they progressed toward the far end, it became increasingly dilapidated. Chunks of stone from the walls lay on the ground, and some sections had crumbled entirely. In addition, pieces of metal roofing were missing.

Perhaps Marc left it that way so casual passersby would think it was abandoned.

"Did you hear that?" Kelly whispered, putting a restraining hand on Emma's arm. Wayne, too, had heard something and he paused, head cocked and listening. The faint sound of a woman's voice floated on the air, snatched away by the breeze swirling down out of the rock outcropping. Wayne nodded and put his finger to his lips, then made a motion with his hand, indicating they should wait. Of course they didn't obey and continued to creep along after the lawman as he tiptoed around the corner of the building.

He froze and then quickly lay down flat, making the rest of the approach on his stomach. As the women drew closer, they saw what had startled him and dropped to the ground also.

The back wall was almost entirely down, lying scattered in a tumble of rocks and rubble. Inside the room, shafts of sunlight poured through a hole in the roof, illuminating Dakota, tied to a chair facing them. Her eyes widened when she spotted her friends, but she quickly looked away before Fiske, guarding her with a gun, noticed. He paced back and forth in front of Dakota, glancing frequently at the dark doorway into the rest of the building. Obviously he was waiting for Marc or Jim Smith to join him.

What now? Emma wondered. She scanned the sky for a sign of the air team Wayne had promised. On the ground beside her, Kelly grabbed her hand and squeezed, obviously just as confused about what to do.

Then she had an idea. Filling her hand with dirt and sand, she rubbed it on her clothes. Then she did the same to Kelly, whispering her plan.

The two of them stood up and walked toward the opening,

not bothering to be quiet. Behind them, Wayne Bryant signaled frantically, but Emma ignored him.

"I really hope someone here can help us," Emma said. "I can't believe the rental car broke down like that."

Fiske stopped his pacing and whirled around, his gun pointed at them. Emma waved, pretending she didn't notice. "Sir? Can you help us? Our car broke down."

Seeing that it was just two unarmed, disheveled women, Fiske tucked the gun into the back of his pants and stepped outside. "You two really shouldn't be here. It's private property."

Emma looked around with a smile, all dimples. "Really? We just need to call roadside assistance. Our phones don't work out here. But you can call for us, right?" She batted her lashes, sensing Dottie Faye's approval as she flirted for all she was worth.

Kelly jumped in. "Our car is out there." She pointed into the desert, and Fiske obediently looked in that direction.

Wayne, finally catching on, was circling around behind Fiske.

"I guess you can't see it from here," Emma said, craning her neck. "It's behind those rocks. We were driving along fine and then all of sudden—hiss! It stopped dead and clouds of steam poured out."

Fiske nodded wisely. "Radiator blew, sounds like."

On cat feet, Wayne approached. "Put your hands up," he said, gun to the back of Fiske's head. "You're under arrest." With the other hand, he removed Fiske's gun from his waistband and tucked it into his pocket.

Fiske raised his hands in the air. "You two were just foolin', huh? There ain't no broken car." He glared at Emma and Kelly.

Emma didn't bother to answer. She and Kelly dashed into the room and quickly untied Dakota, who practically wept with relief at being freed. She gave them big hugs of gratitude. Wayne tied Fiske's hands with plastic handcuffs.

"He killed my cousin," Dakota cried out, rubbing her sore wrists. "I heard Smith say so."

Wayne shook the man's shoulder. "Kidnapping and murder. You're going away for a while." He turned to the women. "Get out of here, and wait in the rocks. You don't want to be in here once the team arrives."

Grabbing Dakota, they climbed back out and headed for high ground. Tucked safely in a good vantage point under an overhanging ledge, they watched as helicopters buzzed overhead and landed outside the pottery factory. Military vehicles approached, announced by clouds of dust. Teams of men brandishing weapons ran into the building from all sides.

Dottie Faye whipped out a video camera and began to film. "I'm gonna upload this to YouTube." She reached down and pulled off her boot with one hand. "Get on the Web and tweet about the big bust going down."

Emma and Kelly exchanged incredulous glances.

Dakota burst out laughing. "Dottie Faye, you are just too much. You must have so much fun with her around," she said to Emma and Kelly.

"There's never a dull moment, that's for sure," Emma said.

"You know you love me, Emma Jane," Dottie Faye said with a smug smile, her gaze never leaving the viewfinder. "The fact that I'm such a great operative is a bonus."

"You're all great detectives," Dakota said. "I can't thank you enough for helping me find out who killed John." She shuddered. "I made a terrible mistake last night and it almost cost me my life."

"You confronted Marc?" Emma guessed.

"Yes. I told him I knew about the forgery. I tried to pretend I was interested in being part of the ring, but I guess he didn't believe me. So early this morning, Fiske and Smith showed up in my room."

"Surely another murder wouldn't help them stay under the radar!" Kelly protested.

Dakota's face was grim. "They weren't going to shoot me. They were planning to throw me down a mine shaft and pretend I had gotten lost and fallen in."

"That's horrible!" Emma cried. A thought struck her. Perhaps Rose's death had been the same—a staged accident, not a moment of passion as they had assumed.

"I'm just glad you found the map. It was the only clue I had time to leave."

The four of them watched as Marc and the other men were brought out of the building, arms cuffed behind them. Wayne Bryant could be seen conferring with the leaders of the SWAT team. It was really over, Emma thought with relief.

Dakota seemed to share her thought as she gave a deep sigh and took Emma's hand. "You'll find out who's responsible for Rose's death too. I just know it. Don't give up."

Emma gazed away from the crime scene and out at the peaceful desert landscape, allowing its beauty and majesty to soothe her heart. "I'll never give up, Rose," she whispered to herself. "I promise."

twenty

Clusters of nodding yellow daffodils lined Kelly's front walk, a perfect touch of spring on this April Easter Day. Emma paused to enjoy them along with the budding leaves on the big maple tree sheltering the Colonial-style house and the robins twittering and pecking while they hopped about on the newly green grass.

Massachusetts was so lush compared to the subtle and much drier beauty of the desert. She'd enjoyed the change in scenery offered by Arizona, especially on the last day when they had a chance to really relax by the resort pool. In fact, the Lone Star Warblers had serenaded them poolside. Bev and her husband appreciated Emma, Kelly and Dottie Faye saving them from what would have been a horrible investment.

Yes, the Arizona sun had been warm. Her nose still had the sunburn to prove it. And the Sedona adventure had taken them another step closer to finding Rose's killer. But it felt good to be back.

A loud honk from the street caught her attention. Dottie Faye, at the wheel of her Cadillac, swung into a spot along the sidewalk. While she watched, her aunt climbed out, stopping to grab a cardboard box from the front passenger seat. Dottie Faye regarded all holidays as an excuse to dress up, and Easter was no exception. She was dressed head to toe in lilac, including a monstrous wide-brimmed hat adorned with silk lilac clusters and a big gauze ribbon. Even her open-toe slingbacks were dyed to match.

"What's that?" she asked as Dottie Faye caught up to her with a clatter of heels. "It's a surprise. I'll tell you inside." Her gaze scanned Emma's outfit—a pale blue sheath and bolero. "You look lovely, sweet pea. You should wear that color more often."

Emma had stepped back to let Dottie Faye go ahead, and when she stopped dead in front of her, Emma almost trod right on her heels. "Dottie Faye!"

Dottie Faye was looking toward the front entrance. "There's another surprise today, Emma Jane, and this one's for you."

Emma followed her gaze to the glass storm door. A familiar little figure stood there, and she jumped up and down when she saw Emma.

"Riley is joining us for dinner?" Riley Hart was the ten-year-old daughter of Dr. Eric Hart, a widower and prime marriage candidate for Emma in Dottie Faye's eyes. "That means ...?" Emma's voice trailed off as Eric joined Riley in the doorway. He held the door wide for them, beaming. Emma noticed how handsome he looked in his gray suit and white shirt. His tie had colorful Easter eggs on it.

"Happy Easter, Dottie Faye. Emma." They returned the greeting and edged past him into Kelly's spacious hallway. Straight ahead was the staircase to the second floor, and through double doors to the left, guests were clustered in the living room. Emma spotted Kelly, her husband and children, Maeve Quigley, Kelly's sister Kathleen, and a uniformed soldier. Kathleen's twin, Sean Quigley, Jr., had made it home from his military assignment for the holiday.

"Look what the Easter bunny brought me." Riley showed Emma a basket filled with chocolate eggs and rabbits and jelly beans, all nestled in green paper grass. "Do you want a bunny?"

"Maybe after dinner," Emma said. "I don't want to spoil

my appetite." She had been surprised to see Eric and suspected Dottie Faye's hand in the invitation, but she had to admit that she adored Riley. And what was a holiday without a child around?

In the living room, Kelly came to give Emma a hug. "I see you're wearing Dakota's earrings," Kelly said. "So am I." As a thank-you, Dakota had given them each a pair of handmade sleeping beauty earrings, consisting of a silver square adorned with a turquoise drop.

Shortly after Emma arrived, dinner was served in the dining room, the antique mahogany table opened up with both leaves to accommodate the group. Maeve, Patrick, and Kelly bustled back and forth to the kitchen, bringing out a huge spiral-cut ham, scalloped and mashed potatoes, fresh spring peas, asparagus, glazed pearl onions, and homemade rolls. Sean, Jr., seated next to his mother, Maeve, was called upon to say grace. Then they all dug into the feast.

"I saw your video on YouTube," Kelly's son, Keith, said to Dottie Faye. "You got tons of hits."

Dottie Faye shrugged casually. "Yes, it went viral, as they say."

"It's too bad you didn't make any progress regarding Rose's case," Eric said to Emma. "But I'm glad you were able to help your friend."

"Me too," Emma said. "We just got an email yesterday from Dakota," she said to the table at large. "She's going to take over her cousin's art gallery. One of her first shows is going to be a selection of Hopi and settler quilts. She's hoping we can advise her."

"She sent me something too," Dottie Faye said. Excusing herself for a moment, she left the table, returning with the mysterious cardboard box. She put it on the sideboard and quickly opened it. Then she pulled out an Anasazi bowl and held it up for everyone to admire.

"Is that real?" Emma blurted out.

"Of course," Dottie Faye said. "And I have the paperwork to prove it." She waved a piece of paper.

"It looks just like the one you bought," Kelly said.

"That's because it is the same one. Wayne Bryant let Dakota have it back, even though it was evidence, and she sent it to me as a thank-you." She leveled a smirk at Emma. "Apparently he was also asking for your email address, Emma Jane."

"That's the FBI agent, right? Maybe he wants to offer you a job," Keith said, his voice rising in excitement.

Emma ducked her head, a hot blush suffusing her cheeks. Why did Dottie Faye say that and right in front of Eric Hart? It must have been on purpose.

Dottie Faye had returned to her seat and was now nattering away about Emma's popularity with cowboys and how she'd been the belle of the line dance.

"I guess I better take riding lessons," Eric whispered to Emma.

"I'm thinking about a visit to the shooting range to brush up," Emma whispered back. "Bless her interfering little heart."

They both burst out laughing. Yes, Emma was glad to be home.

Mystery Sampler Quilt

Create your own mystery sampler quilt with blocks designed by Emma and Kelly and inspired by each book in the series! You'll find a Cotton & Grace block pattern in every Annie's Quilted Mysteries book. At the end of the series, the last pattern will include finishing instructions that will tell you how to stitch the unique blocks together to create a beautiful, one-of-a-kind quilt.

Rustic Lodge

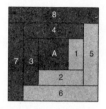

Rustic Lodge
12" x 12" Finished Block

Specifications
Finished Block Size: 12" x 12"
Skill Level: Beginner

Cutting

From Light Fabric:
Cut 1 each:
   2½" x 4½" strip 1
   2½" x 6½" strip 2
   2½" x 8½" strip 5
   2½" x 10½" strip 6

From Dark Fabric:
Cut 1 (4½") A square.
Cut 1 each:
   2½" x 6½" strip 3
   2½" x 8½" strip 4
   2½" x 10½" strip 7
   2½" x 12½" strip 8

Assembly

1. Stitch strip 1 to right side edge of A square (Figure 1). Press seam toward 1.

Figure 1   **Figure 2**

2. Stitch strip 2 to bottom of A-1 unit (Figure 2). Press seam toward 2.

3. Stitch strip 3 to left side of A-1-2 unit (Figure 3). Press seam toward 3.

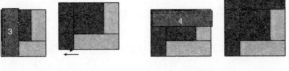

Figure 3 **Figure 4**

4. Stitch strip 4 to top of unit (Figure 4). Press seam toward 4.

5. Continue adding strips to the unit clockwise in numerical order and pressing seams toward rectangles. ***Note:*** *It is easy to make a mistake in the stitching order. Turn pieced unit so that the most recently added strip is closest to you when placed under the presser foot, then add the next rectangle to the side under the presser foot.*

HELPFUL HINTS

• Choose light and dark fabrics for this block. Use scraps from other projects or purchase fat eighths (9" x 22") or fat quarters (18" x 22") to make one sample block.

• Cut individual pieces from scraps, or cut strips and then individual pieces from strips if using yardage or large pieces of fabric. For example, to cut several 2½" squares, cut a 2½"-wide strip the width of the fabric. Subcut the strip into 2½" squares.

• Use a ¼"-wide seam allowance for all seams and stitch right sides together.

• For more detailed help with quilting techniques, go to QuiltersWorld.com and choose Quilting Basics under Quilt Essentials, or consult a complete quilting guide. Your local library will probably have several on hand that you can review before purchasing one.

Learn more about Annie's fiction books at

AnniesFiction.com

- Access your e-books
- Discover exciting new series
- Read sample chapters
- Watch video book trailers
- Share your feedback

We've designed the Annie's Fiction website especially for you!

Plus, manage your account online!

- Check your account status
- Make payments online
- Update your address

ANNIE'S ATTIC
MYSTERIES®

CREATIVE WOMAN
MYSTERIES®

Annie's
Quilted
Mysteries™

Annie's
Mysteries

Unraveled™

Visit us at AnniesFiction.com

COMING SOON!

UNSAVORY NOTIONS

Emma, Kelly, and Dottie Faye next head to
Amish country in search of their next suspect,
Hannah Beiler. Hannah was on *rumspringa*
when she took Rose Peterson's class.

Is it possible that the nonviolent Amish
community is harboring a murderer?

Don't miss the next book in this
exciting new series from
Annie's Quilted Mysteries!